Mills & Boon
Best Seller Romance

A chance to read and collect some of the best-loved novels from Mills & Boon—the world's largest publisher of romantic fiction.

Every month, four titles by favourite Mills & Boon authors will be re-published in the *Best Seller Romance* series.

A list of other titles in the *Best Seller Romance* series can be found at the end of this book.

Anne Hampson

BELOVED RAKE

MILLS & BOON LIMITED
LONDON · TORONTO

All the characters in this book have no existence outside the imagination of the Author, and have no relation whatsoever to anyone bearing the same name or names. They are not even distantly inspired by any individual known or unknown to the Author, and all the incidents are pure invention.

The text of this publication or any part thereof may not be reproduced or transmitted in any form or by any means, electronic or mechanical, including photocopying, recording, storage in an information retrieval system, or otherwise, without the written permission of the publisher.

This book is sold subject to the condition that it shall not, by way of trade or otherwise, be lent, resold, hired out or otherwise circulated without the prior consent of the publisher in any form of binding or cover other than that in which it is published and without a similar condition including this condition being imposed on the subsequent purchaser.

First published 1972
Australian copyright 1982
Philippine copyright 1982
This edition 1982

© Harlequin Enterprises B.V. 1972

ISBN 0 263 73886 8

Set in Linotype Baskerville 10 on 11½ pt.
02–0582

Made and printed in Great Britain by
Richard Clay (The Chaucer Press) Ltd,
Bungay, Suffolk

CHAPTER ONE

SHE had run away—away from her father and authority and the handsome young Greek whom her father had chosen as her husband. She had only been told he was handsome, for as yet she had not set eyes on him. They were all there now—Father and Aunt Agni, and Phivos and his parents—discussing the dowry while she, Serra, was all alone in an adjoining room—or she should have been!—awaiting the verdict of Phivos's parents. If all was settled to everyone's satisfaction then her father would come for her, with the intention of introducing her to her future husband.

What a shock they would all receive! But Serra's satisfaction was short-lived; she had run from them, but where could she go? Like bees when they swarm she had rested not far from her home before making the second—and final—flight into freedom. A six-drachmae bus ride had brought her from her father's flower-bedecked villa outside Athens to the Acropolis, where she sat, on one of the marble steps forming the base of the Parthenon, the world's most spectacular and famous building. Her knees were drawn up, her chin resting forlornly in her hands. She gazed with unseeing eyes at the camera-snapping group of people listening in awe-struck wonderment to the guide who, in husky tones, was giving them a brief outline of the history of the site. No one took the slightest notice of Serra, sitting there alone on the steps of the great Temple of Athena, and she wallowed in her misery quite undisturbed. What was to be done? Vaguely she had England as her objective, because her mother had been English—that was why Serra spoke the language so well, with the merest trace of an accent which an English lady had once described as delectable. England, and freedom. If she ever did get there what a time she would have! After the restrictions she had endured since her mother's death, Serra felt she would just go on and on having her fling. A deep sigh, and a hand stealing to the pocket of her skirt. Three hundred drachmae... rather less than four English pounds.

Suddenly she swallowed the saliva collecting on her tongue, aware that her inside held half a dozen caged butterflies, but aghast at the idea that she was about to be sick. *Sick*—not here on the steps of the Parthenon! It would be sacrilege! The little knot of people were some distance away now, and she would not be seen, but.... Unsteadily she rose to her feet, but her legs felt like jelly.

'Sit still a moment,' begged a lively male voice, and Serra glanced up to see a young man focusing a camera on her—or so it would seem. 'It'll help to fix the perspective.' He was taking the temple, she realized.

'I c-can't——' A hand went to her mouth; she wondered if she looked as green as she felt. 'I'm g-going to be s-sick!'

'How revolting!' Another voice, deep and cultured and edged with a sort of pained inflection. 'Better leave your picture until another time, Charles.' The man made to walk away.

'No—wait, Dirk—the child's ill——'

'My dear Charles,' drawled the voice, 'not again! Wherever you go you seem to find a damsel in distress, as you so cheerfully term them. Come on, the picture can wait.'

'Perhaps, but the girl——' He looked down at her. 'I say, are you really going to be si— Er—do you feel dreadfully ill?'

Serra nodded, managing to flash an indignant glance at Dirk, who was clearly impatient to move on. What a tall man!—and lean and sort of—sinewed——

'Oh,' she groaned. 'Yes, I'm feeling dreadfully ill.' She swayed slightly and Charles caught hold of her arm.

'The poodle door's over there.' He pointed vaguely. Dirk frowned. Clearly he was becoming exceedingly irritated by his friend's interest in Serra.

'Poodle door...?' She glanced in the direction indicated.

'You know, the door with the poodle on it,' Charles elucidated. 'The poodle is leading a woman along.'

'Oh....' Serra nodded, enlightened. 'Yes, I'll——' She stopped and looked appealingly at Charles, her big brown eyes moist, her lip quivering. 'I don't think I can get there. Will you turn your head, please?'

'For heaven's sake, Charles, come away! The girl wants privacy.'

But Charles had no intention of leaving Serra. Passing her a huge handkerchief, he spoke soothingly to her, at the same time leading her away from the steps. His frank round face was troubled, his eyes shadowed. But they had barely taken half a dozen steps when Serra exclaimed in relief,

'It's gone off me now!' She still felt green, but her stomach had settled. 'I'm awfully sorry; it was the anxiety. You see, I'm in trouble.'

'You——' Charles's eyes moved automatically over her slender figure. Dirk's eyes made a similar move.

'Not what you think, Charles,' he drawled. 'Greek girls never do.'

'Never?' Charles's eyes opened wide. 'Then how——'

7

Serra interrupted, oblivious of what the conversation was about.

'I'm not Greek. My mother was English.'

'Was?'

'She died three years ago, when I was fifteen.' She gave a little gulp, but was relieved to find it was nothing serious. Thank goodness she wasn't going to be sick, after all. 'I've run away from home,' she informed them, directing her gaze at Dirk to see what effect this dramatic piece of news would have on him. Stifling a yawn, he said,

'Are you expecting our congratulations? Running away from home is the done thing these days, isn't it?'

'Not with Greek girls,' she retorted indignantly.

'You've just said you're not Greek,' Charles reminded her, and his friend gave an audible sigh of impatience.

'My father is, and that's why I've run away. He's always choosing husbands for me——'

'Always?' cut in Charles, frowning. 'Do you have more than one husband in Greece?'

'Don't be silly, of course we don't!' She stopped and glanced at Dirk. Why did he appear so bored? He didn't seem at all sympathetic about her terrible plight—not like his nice friend, Charles. 'Father chose one boy for me last year and I refused to meet him, then a few months ago he chose another, and I wouldn't meet him either. But this time Father said I must marry Phivos, and they were arranging it when I ran away.' Encouraged by Charles's interest, she went on to explain the procedure, ending by saying that had her mother been alive the situation would not have arisen because her mother had always promised that Serra should find her own husband.

'Well,' said Charles after a little pause during which

he digested all this, 'I don't blame you for running away. Have you decided where you're going?'

'I want to get to England, but I've only got three hundred drachmae.'

To her surprise Dirk's eyes suddenly kindled with amusement, and he appeared slightly interested now, although he made no comment on this astounding admission.

'You'll not get far on that.' Charles shook his head. 'I should go back home if I were you.' Serra made a feeble protest by shaking her head and Charles then asked what she had against this young man her father had chosen for her.

'I don't really know,' she frankly admitted, 'because I've never seen him, but I didn't like his voice.'

'His voice?' Dirk spoke at last. 'That's nothing.'

'You have to live with your husband's voice,' she pointed out. 'Just imagine listening all your life to a voice that grates on your nerves. You have a beautiful voice,' she added irrelevantly.

Charles grinned, but Dirk maintained an impassive countenance. She examined him for a moment. He was extraordinarily handsome, she decided without any hesitation. Lean features with faintly hollowed cheeks; clear-cut lines to a jaw that was rather too stern and set. Still, she mused, he did seem to have features that went together, as it were, and the whole was most attractive despite the slight austerity that looked out from his piercing brown eyes. His bearing had arrested her from the first because it reminded her of the mental picture she had drawn of the English aristocrat. Her mother used to tell her about these people, and how they lived in mansions standing in magnificent grounds and had lots of servants to wait on them. Serra wondered if Charles and Dirk belonged to this exalted class. If only she could get to England! It must be a most exciting place in which to live. And the freedom—oh, what a time she could have!

'Will you help me to get to England?' The question seemed to come from nowhere—for Serra could not believe that she had asked it, not of a complete stranger.

'Me?' Emphatically Charles shook his head. 'You must go home, little girl.'

She nodded bleakly.

'If only an Englishman would offer for me,' she sighed. 'I think my father would be only too glad to let me go, for he said only yesterday that if I refused Phivos he'd never get me off his hands because no one else would ever offer for me.' She looked up at Charles, totally unaware of her appeal ... or that her words had sparked off an idea in Charles's mind. 'You see, it's already all over my village that I've refused two—well, it'll be three now—and they'll all be saying I'm too proud and so no one will allow their son to offer for me.'

'Charles,' said Dirk, bored by this pathetic story, 'do you move on with me or do I return to the hotel alone?'

'Are you going?' The low-toned question was directed at Charles, but Serra was looking at his friend. He wasn't nice at all, she thought. So superior and aloof. How had a charming young man like Charles come to choose him for a friend? 'Are you on holiday?' she asked, handing back the handkerchief to Charles.

'Just beginning it,' he smiled. 'We're here for a week and then we're going on to Beirut.'

'You must belong to the rich English?' Serra was trying her best to keep them with her a little while longer, for she was becoming more and more frightened of what she had done, and the company kept her from falling into total abject misery. To her surprise her words had a remarkable effect on both Charles and Dirk, who exchanged glances that could only be described as exceedingly strange. 'Have I said something wrong?' she inquired apologetically. Charles shook his head, but seemed suddenly to become lost in thought. 'Oh, dear,' groaned Serra, putting a hand to her stomach. 'The—the poodle door!' She started to run, aware that Charles was calling after her; vaguely she heard him say,

'We'll wait for you—by the little temple over there. Nike, I think they call it.'

In less than ten minutes Serra was standing by the Temple of Nike, feeling utterly lost. They had gone—and she had been as quick as she could. But she had known that nasty Dirk would take this opportunity of getting his friend away from her. For about five minutes she walked about, searching for the two men while fully convinced that Dirk had forced Charles to hurry off so that they would never see her again. She would have had to go home in any case, she thought, but if only they had stayed with her a little while longer. It was so exciting to be free to talk to a man as she had talked to Charles, even though she knew that, should she be seen by anyone in her village, she would be ruined for life, because in Greece a girl must never be seen with a man before her marriage. But she had not been afraid; no one in her village would be here. This place was for the tourists, and many of the natives had never even seen it—except on picture postcards, of course, because they were on sale everywhere.

Serra had been wandering away from the temple,

walking aimlessly as she thought of the two men and of her problem and of England, where she longed to be. And it was with faint surprise that she found herself near the Erectheum. She sat down on some stones, biting her lip hard because the tears were very close.

Voices! Suddenly alert, Serra sat straight up and looked over her shoulder. But the two men were sitting round the corner from her, out of sight. Their voices reached her plainly. Dirk sounded impatient as he said,

'I had an idea what was in your mind the moment she mentioned the rich English——'

'I knew you did; I could tell by the way you looked at me.'

'Well, as I've said, if you want the girl rescuing you can rescue her yourself.'

'You're crazy! Here's the answer to your problem, being handed out to you on a plate, and you ignore it.'

'You seem to be forgetting Clarice.'

'You know very well you don't want to marry her. If you did you'd have done it long ago. Why, everyone knows you're leaving it until the last minute just to see if someone better turns up.'

'Thanks; you're not very flattering.'

'Oh, I know you could have plenty—but not the right sort. They'll interfere with your freedom; your carefree life will come to an end. But just you mark my words, Clarice won't be any easy-going, docile wife. She's possessive already, so you can expect trouble in plenty if you marry her. No, Dirk, a meek and timid little Greek girl's what you want. She won't interfere or make claims on your time. She's been brought up to recognize the superiority of man and she wouldn't dream of stepping out of place. If you marry this child you'll be able to carry on as you always have; you won't even *know* you're married!'

'Anyone would think your concern was all for me,' returned Dirk with a laugh.

'But of course it is——'

'Your concern, Charles, is with the damsel in distress. I know you, remember. Your heart's too soft.'

Serra sat there, dazed by this conversation, but tensed also, and she was aware of the dampness on her forehead and in the palms of her hands, which were tightly clutched in her lap. She had no idea of the true content of the conversation, but she did realize that Dirk had a problem, and that the problem concerned a wife. And Charles was suggesting that Dirk solve that problem by marrying her, Serra. If only it had been Charles who had the problem, she thought dejectedly, then he would not have hesitated to marry her.

'Perhaps my heart is too soft,' Charles was saying, 'but it's better than having a heart which is too hard.' Dirk merely laughed again and Charles went on, his voice tinged with anxiety, 'I wonder if she's worse than we thought——'

'I didn't think anything, Charles,' intervened Dirk gently.

'All right, all right,' from Charles, impatiently. 'What I was trying to say was, where is the child? Why hasn't she come back before now?'

'Gone off home, I expect—back to an irate papa and an affronted fiancé.'

'I don't believe it; the child was distraught. Besides, she told you she couldn't stand the fellow's voice—she liked yours,' he digressed, adding that this in itself was an omen. 'I'm going to look for her,' he ended, and Serra heard the crunch of stones as he rose to his feet. 'The poor child might be staggering about, all alone——'

'I'm here,' said Serra, hurriedly jumping to her feet. She didn't want to lose Charles again, at least, not for a little while. 'You said the Temple of Nike.' She had moved to the corner of the building; Dirk was still sitting down, but he began to ease himself off the broken column on which he sat. After a moment he was regarding her through narrowed eyes.

'Isn't this the Temple of Nike?' Charles was asking, casting a vague glance at the caryatids.

'It's the Erectheum.' Serra's head was raised to meet Dirk's searching gaze. *He* had known this was not the Temple of Nike, she decided. 'I thought I'd lost you,' she said to Charles in quivering tones.

'Mistake. But no harm done.' Charles stared into her face. 'White—very white. You'd better come with us and we'll get you a drink.'

Serra opened her mouth to thank him, but Dirk spoke before she could do so.

'How long have you been here?' His voice was clipped and stern-edged. Serra blushed hotly.

'Not l-long...' She tailed off because it was impossible to lie while those piercing eyes were fixed upon her.

'How much did you hear?'

'Oh, I say, Dirk,' protested Charles indignantly. 'The girl wouldn't deliberately listen!'

'She listened to the arrangements being made for her marriage.'

Serra's head came up at this. The man was downright rude!

'How much did you hear?' he asked again, and when she failed to answer he repeated his question. Serra knew she would have to answer in the end, so she admitted she had been sitting round the corner for about five minutes.

Charles looked quite put out by this and glanced from Serra to Dirk, anxiously scanning his face.

'We must get her that drink,' he murmured, less buoyancy in his voice now. 'She's not fully recovered yet——' Breaking off, he turned to Serra. 'What's your name? I can't keep saying her and she.'

'Serra Costalos.'

'Serra? So your mother didn't give you an English name, then?'

Serra shook her head.

'She liked Serra,' was all she said. Her head was aching; she thought it must be nerves, and she felt she might be better for the drink Charles had promised to get her. 'Are we going to the *taverna*?'

Charles looked rather uncertainly at Dirk.

'If you want to go back?' he began. 'I'll take Serra for a drink.'

But to the surprise of both Serra and Charles, Dirk agreed to accompany them to the *taverna*.

Serra glanced round as they entered; her apprehension was not lost on Dirk and he asked her what was wrong.

'If anyone should see me with you two my reputation would be ruined,' she answered unthinkingly.

'It would?' Dirk raised his brows and Serra flushed again.

'I didn't mean you two particularly,' she hastily assured him. 'In Greece a girl must not be seen with men.'

'What sort of a drink do you want?' Strangely it was Dirk who put the question. Serra said she would have soda water. 'Do they have it here?' Dirk added.

'Yes, I think so.'

Dirk and Charles had beer. When the drinks were

brought Dirk spoke again, his words bringing a swift expectant tingle to Serra and a look of disbelief to Charles's eyes.

'This offering that men do here—what exactly happens?'

'The man sees the girl—it might be that he passes her house when she's in the garden, or he might see her sitting on the patio of an evening, with her female relatives, doing her embroidery. On the other hand, one of his relatives might have seen the girl, and thought her suitable for their son or nephew. Then negotiations begin between the two families.' Serra stopped to sip her drink and Charles said, avoiding his friend's gaze,

'What do these negotiations entail?'

'Well, the boy's parents want to know the value of her dowry, and the girl's parents want to know if the boy is good, and they send out all the girl's relatives to discover whether or not there are any scandals attached to the boy.'

'Scandals?' almost ejaculated Charles, and Serra stared interrogatingly at him. He seemed to have something stuck in his throat. 'Well, that appears to be that,' he remarked as an accompaniment to his friend's laughter. After a moment Dirk said quietly,

'You said the boy offers for the girl—at least, you've told us this Phivos offered for you. Is that right?'

'Yes. After he saw me—it was in a shop—he told his parents and they let him offer for me.'

Dirk's laughter had faded just as swiftly as it had arisen, and for a long while he remained deep in thought, although now and then he would look hard at Serra, as if he wished to get a better picture of her. His eyes seemed to take in everything, from her shining brown hair to her flawless face with its classical features and contours, and to her long neck, then his glance moved lower to the enchanting curves and tiny waist.

She sat very still, her mind on what she had heard. Was Dirk considering offering for her? she wondered, her feelings mixed. Freedom ... but if only it had been Charles....

'Dirk,' ventured Charles slowly as the silence continued, 'are you considering offering for Serra?'

At this outright question Dirk frowned, though his eyes never left Serra's face.

'You don't appear to be surprised by my friend's question,' he observed in a rather lazy tone.

'I heard what you were saying,' she reminded him, her gaze wide and honest. And then she too became venturesome as she added, 'Why must you have a wife?'

'Must?' curtly.

'It's obvious that you don't really want one....' Her sudden intake of breath portrayed enlightenment. 'Is it a marriage of convenience?' she asked, going on to say she had heard about those.

'You have?' in an astonished voice from Charles. 'I can't imagine them occurring in Greece.'

'Is it because of a job?' Serra asked, ignoring Charles's intervention.

Dirk's frown deepened uncomprehendingly.

'Job? What do you mean?'

She hesitated. Somehow she could not imagine Dirk requiring a job—and yet he must earn his living somehow. Of course, he could belong to the landed gentry her mother used to talk about. Both he and Charles appeared to be very rich. Recalling what had passed between the two men she now had another idea. But she did not voice it, at least, not yet.

'Sometimes if a man applies for a particular job they ask him if he's married, and if he isn't then they won't employ him.'

Dirk's lips curved faintly at her explanation. He shook his head.

'It's not a job,' was all he said.

'Is it a will, then?' she asked, and this time it was Charles who smiled.

'Right second time! Clever girl.' That he would have gone on to explain was evident, but he caught the rather darkling look in his friend's eye and closed his mouth.

Nevertheless, Dirk was now extremely interested in the idea which had originally come from his friend. Serra, highly intelligent, could see this, and while she wanted to exploit the situation she was at a loss as to how to go about it. She had been given hope and felt that if she were now disappointed she would never recover. Already she saw herself in England, freed from all restriction and able to do just whatever she liked. She thought of what Charles had said about Dirk's being able to carry on as he always had, and Serra knew it would suit her very well to have it that way. Had she been married to a Greek it would have been like that, for he would very soon resume his custom of going about with his friends—and having a girl-friend, should the idea appeal to him. But whereas in Greece she, as a wife, would remain at home every day and evening, doing her embroidery and chatting with the other female members of the household, in England she would be able to go out and enjoy herself. And it would not matter if she had boy-friends—not if, as Charles had suggested, Dirk wanted to carry on as if he weren't married at all.

Still endeavouring to find some means of helping to

strengthen the idea now becoming rooted in Dirk's mind, Serra was lost in silence, scarcely aware that the two men were talking. But one word caught her ear that made her look up.

'You have a mother?' She was thinking of her own mother, and the terrible feeling of loss when she died. If Dirk had a mother, and she was like Serra's own mother.... Serra put a brake on her thoughts. Dirk had not offered for her, and she had the dismal conviction that, once away from her and back in his hotel, he would regard the whole idea as ridiculous. If only she could persuade him to offer immediately, then she would be safe, for she somehow knew he would never change his mind once the offer was made.

'Yes, I have a mother.' Dirk's eyes regarded her with a sardonic expression. 'What interest is that to you?' he then added, and Serra looked at him with a frank and open gaze.

'I know you're wondering whether or not to offer for me,' she said, abandoning all attempts to find some subtle way of persuasion. 'I would be grateful if you did, and I would be very good, and not interfere—as your friend said, up there, when I listened.'

'There you are,' interposed Charles brightly. 'Serra's promised to be good and not interfere. What more do you want?'

Dirk appeared to be extremely amused now. Certainly he was not in the least perturbed at the idea of having to get married. He seemed to have accepted the dictates of whoever had made the will in a most philosophic manner, which was sensible, thought Serra, for there was nothing he could do about it. She looked at him and tried to guess his age, wondering if he had to be married by a certain birthday. He would be about twenty-eight, she surmised, and Charles was about a year younger.

'Are you quite sure your father would welcome me as a suitor——?' He stopped, because Serra had begun to tremble so violently that the glass in her hand was shaking and its contents spilling on to the table. 'Are you ill again?' he asked.

She shook her head; Charles took the glass from her and placed it on the table.

'No, I'm not ill—only excited. Are you really going to offer for me?' And without waiting for an answer, 'Yes, Father will welcome you, and I'm sure he'll let me marry you.' She then remembered Charles's reaction when she had previously mentioned scandals and, suspecting that there had been scandals in Dirk's family, she hastily added, 'Because of your being English, and not living here, my father won't be able to investigate your—your....' She tailed off and Dirk continued for her, his tones dry-edged but also faintly amused,

'My past? Is that what you were about to say?' She blushed and nodded and Dirk turned to his friend. 'You really should practise more tact, Charles. The child is wondering if it's a rake who's contemplating offering for her.'

'Oh, I don't mind at all,' said Serra obligingly. 'If you are a rake, then you must carry on. All I want is to get to England and—and enjoy myself.' She suddenly had doubts. 'Would I be able to enjoy myself?' So naïve she looked that, in spite of his hardness and lack of interest in her as anything but an object of usefulness, Dirk found himself feeling rather sorry for her.

'Certainly you would be able to enjoy yourself. You could do exactly as you liked.'

Her eyes glowed, and she began to tremble again as her excitement got the better of her once more.

'It sounds wonderful. You have no idea how I've wanted to get to England! My mother was always talking about it, you see, and she said that when I was older she would try to take me on a visit.'

'Why haven't you been on a visit before now?'

'We never had the money. Father's not rich, and that's why he'll be glad to get me off his hands——' She stopped, then asked breathlessly, 'Would you want the dowry?'

Dirk laughed then, and she thought he did not seem so very austere after all.

'No, I shouldn't require the dowry.'

'Then my father would most certainly accept you as my—did you say suitor?' and when Dirk nodded, 'Yes, he'd be delighted because he can't really afford the dowry.'

'Have you no relatives in England?' Charles asked, flicking a glance at his friend.

'None that I know of. Mother was an only child and her parents are dead. I might have some cousins several times removed,' she added as an afterthought.

'Well,' said Charles in a satisfied voice, 'it all seems quite plain sailing to me.'

Serra's eyes were on Dirk as she waited in a sort of agonized silence for him to speak.

'I'll think it over,' he murmured thoughtfully at last, and smiled as her face fell.

'You'll change your mind,' she returned bleakly, seeing all her hopes shattered.

'I haven't yet made up my mind so I can hardly change it,' he told her drily, and she turned beseeching eyes to Charles.

'Will you marry me?' she begged. 'As I've said, I'll be very good—and meek,' she added, remembering that he himself had used that word.

'Me!' ejaculated Charles and Dirk said, still in the same dry tone,

'Why not, Charles? After all, it's your idea that the child be rescued.'

'But it's you who is desperately in need of a wife,' his friend was quick to point out.

'Not desperately. I can, as you know, fall back on Clarice.'

Charles made a disgusted gesture with his hand.

'She'll not be meek, I've already told you that. She'll make demands on you, whereas Serra here has been brought up to know her place. Isn't that right?' He looked at Serra, who nodded vigorously.

'Yes, indeed. Here in Greece I would not be allowed to interfere in my husband's doings and so I'd never dream of doing so if I was married to you.' Her glance, which embraced them both, brought laughter to Dirk's eyes.

'Which one of us would you prefer to use?' he asked, watching her closely.

'Use?'

'Don't use a word like that!' interposed Charles indignantly, and immediately employed it himself. 'You'd be using each other, and both gaining enormously in the process.'

'I take it that you yourself don't have any desire to get married?'

Charles frowned.

'I'm not ready to marry yet,' he admitted, rather defensively.

'Nor am I, for that matter.'

'You must, though,' put in Serra eagerly, and again Dirk laughed.

'Yes, child, I must....' He tailed off and Serra had the gratifying impression that had he continued he would have said, 'And it might just as well be to you.'

Two men got up to dance; the performance consisted of the usual lively kicking and jumping and for a few minutes Dirk and Charles drank their beer in silence, watching the men. Serra became impatient, but felt she must not speak. She was on pins as she watched the beer going down in the glasses. Would they order again?—or would Dirk decide to leave the *taverna* without having come to any definite decision? His eyes were thoughtful, she noticed, surmising that he was still considering the matter of marriage to her. If only he knew just what it meant to her. But he would not think of that; he would think only of himself, she felt sure.

At last he gave a small sigh and immediately her dejection vanished.

'Have you decided?' she couldn't help asking, raising her big eyes to his as he turned his head. '*Please*— Mr—Mr . . . ?'

'Morgan's the name——' A long moment of silence and then, 'But you can call me Dirk.'

Her eyes opened very wide.

'You're going to offer for me, then?' she quivered. 'Oh, thank you very much!'

Charles's attention, having been brought from the dancers, was now turned upon his friend.

'You mean it?' he asked.

'Mean what? I haven't said anything that I can recall.'

'Please don't keep me in suspense,' Serra entreated, on the point of tears. 'I promise to be very good, and obliging. As your friend has said, you'll never know you're married. It will be much better than being married to this Clarice,' she persevered. 'She's English and she wouldn't let you do as you like, as I would.'

Dirk's brows had risen while she spoke and she wondered fearfully whether in her desperate attempt to further her cause she had in fact damaged it. However, to her surprise and relief he allowed her words to pass without comment. Charles also betrayed relief at this and asked Dirk if he would like another beer.

'No, I don't think so.' He glanced at his watch. 'It's time we were getting back to the hotel for lunch.' He looked at Serra and added, in a rather casual voice, 'When will it be convenient for me to visit your father?'

She could not speak for a long moment. It wasn't true—it couldn't be true!

'Now—at once,' she replied when eventually she had convinced herself that it was true. England! And freedom! What a time she meant to have! 'We can catch a bus just outside here——'

'Bus?' frowned Charles with a slight shudder. 'We always travel by taxi.'

'We can get a taxi——' She stopped, for Dirk was shaking his head.

'As I've said,' he commented, rising from his chair, 'it's time we were getting back to the hotel. You can give me your address, child, and I shall call on your father this afternoon.'

Her face fell.

'Not now?' she faltered, still afraid that, after giving the matter more serious thought, he would change his mind.

'Not now.' Dirk produced a piece of paper and a pen. 'Your address.'

She wrote it down with trembling fingers.

'Please come,' she whispered, handing him the paper and the pen. 'I have a dreadful fear that you'll change your mind.'

To her surprise a smile softened the hard outline of his mouth.

'I never break my word,' he assured her, and she knew he meant it. Nevertheless she suggested she wait outside the hotel while he had his lunch, and then they could go together and see her father. She had stood up and her head was tilted right back as she looked up at him.

'Father will be so angry with me for running away,' she explained. 'And I'll feel much more comfortable if you are there....' She tailed off as he again shook his head.

'Go home; tell your father you've met me and that I intend coming to—er—offer for you this afternoon. No, don't interrupt. You would have been forced to go home in any case, and you must do so now. Your father will undoubtedly be very angry with you,' he added without much interest, 'but the fact that you have found yourself a husband should in some way soften his ill-humour—that is, if as you say, he is anxious to get you married.'

'He is certainly anxious to get me married, but—oh, I don't know if I can face his anger!' Dirk merely made an impatient gesture and she went on, 'You see, it isn't allowed for a girl to be with a man, and I don't know if I dare tell him. I wish you would come with me.'

'It will hardly matter that you've been with me if I'm willing to marry you,' he pointed out, trying to keep his patience.

'Perhaps he'll beat the poor child,' put in Charles anxiously, but Serra shook her head at this suggestion.

'He'll just rave and storm and say I've disgraced the whole family.'

'You can put up with that, surely? I'll be there just as soon as I've had my lunch. Besides, your father will require a little time in which to get acclimatized to the idea of your marrying an Englishman. Now, go home—and don't look so dejected. I shan't let you down. Incidentally,' he added as the thought occurred to him, 'there's no need for you to tell your father the details. Just say that I saw you and liked you, and that I've said I intend offering for you. That would be all that would be required had I been a Greek, you said?'

'Yes, that's all you'd have to do.'

'Your father won't say you've let the family down when he learns of Dirk's situation,' Charles put in, adding, despite the rather glowering glance he received from his friend, 'He's very rich—or will be when he's married—and you'll be living in a big house.'

Serra brightened, but said her father would naturally require some credentials. These would be available, Dirk assured her and with that she was again ordered to go home, which she did, bravely prepared to face her irate father, sustained as she now was by the sure knowledge that she would soon be free.

CHAPTER TWO

AFTER the first flare-up it was, strangely, Aunt Agni who continued to pour out invective, and not Serra's father. Aunt Agni declared Serra to be utterly ruined, for someone was bound to have seen her with this man.

'But I keep telling you, he wants to marry me.'

'Nonsense! He'll never come here! Englishmen—they're all the same! Flirts, they are, and that's all he was doing with you! Flirting! Where did you go? Tell me at once!'

'We only went into a *taverna*——'

'*Taverna!*' exclaimed Aunt Agni, throwing up her arms in horror. '*Good* girls *never* frequent *tavernas*!'

'There were two of them——'

'Two! Oh, Elias, say something to this shameless daughter of yours, for I can't find words to express my utter disgust!'

'You appear to have found many words, Agni,' said Mr Costalos, frowning at her. She had come to housekeep for him on the death of his wife, whom she had never really liked, simply because she was English. 'Please go away and leave this matter to me.'

'Very well.' She marched to the door. 'But mark my words, the man will not turn up, so you can forget about marrying Serra off so easily. In fact, you'll never marry her off at all now, because she's ruined—utterly and irreparably ruined!'

Serra stood there before her father; it was a long while before he said,

'Sit down, child, and tell me all about this man who

says he's coming here this afternoon to offer for you.'

But her aunt's words had gone deep, and now that Serra was in her home Dirk Morgan seemed quite unreal. He would not come, she told herself one moment, while the next moment she was hearing his firm voice saying that he never broke his word.

'We met on the Acropolis, as I've said. He was with Charles, his friend,——'

'You picked him up?'

'Picked him up?' They spoke in Greek and Serra took that quite literally. 'I don't know what you mean?'

'It's a typical English expression. In England they meet like that. It's quite disgusting.'

She still remained rather in the dark, and so she ignored that and went on to tell her father all that had happened, without of course mentioning the real reason why Dirk wanted to marry her.

'He promised faithfully he'd come,' she ended in a desperate tone. 'He will come—I know he will!'

'Are you trying to convince me, or yourself?' Her father's voice had lost its anger; he was pained, and exceedingly disappointed in his daughter. 'It's the English blood in your veins,' he added, shaking his head.

'I know he'll come,' she said again, but in a much more subdued voice. Should he not come she was, as Aunt Agni had asserted, utterly ruined. She would be regarded as unchaste by all her relatives, and by all the village, in fact. When she went out all would stare, then look the other way. That was how it was in Greece.

'I sincerely hope you are right, my child, for if this man was indeed flirting with you, and is not serious, then I don't know what's to become of you. We shall

all have to hang our heads in shame for the rest of our lives.'

'You don't mind my marrying him, then?'

'Mind? Serra, it is my one fervent wish that this Dirk will indeed want to marry you.'

She said nothing, but her relief could be seen in her eyes, for she had been slightly troubled that her father would object to her going so far away. Yet she need not have worried because all that concerned him was that he should get her off his hands, so avoiding the shame which threatened to descend upon the whole family.

Her father wanted to know more about Dirk, but there was little Serra could tell him, except that he was rich. This was received with interest, but only briefly, for her father made the firm assertion that the man was just amusing himself with her. Why should a wealthy English tourist want to marry a girl like her? he wanted to know. Here again Serra could not satisfy him and all she could do was advise her father to wait until Dirk arrived.

'You seem so sure he will arrive——' Mr Costalos shook his head. 'Time will show, my daughter, time will show.'

Two hours later Serra was standing by her bedroom window, her heart in her feet. He was not coming. How could she have been so foolish? And what had she been thinking of to talk to the men in the first place, so bringing such disgrace on her family and herself? If she had not been so unhappy she would never have dreamed of talking to strange men. 'It was owing to my feeling ill,' she tried to excuse herself, but she admitted there really was no excuse. Tears moistened her lashes, and within seconds she was weeping as if her heart would break. What was to become of her?

A spinster's life, spent with a father and an aunt who would persistently remind her of the disgrace. The tears poured forth until her eyes were swollen and her cheeks like fire. 'I wish I were dead,' she whispered tragically. 'Oh, please let me die——' Miraculously her tears ceased and she didn't want to die at all. 'He's come!—I knew he'd come!' The taxi had stopped; Dirk alighted and paid the driver. Serra's bedroom was on the ground floor and she ran to the door and listened. Dirk introducing himself to her father. Then silence as they entered the sitting-room. She could not go in to them, for the offer must not be made in her presence. She glanced at the clock every two minutes for the next half hour. What were they talking about? Why hadn't her father come for her? Perhaps something had gone wrong—but there was nothing which could go wrong, she told herself desperately.

'Serra!' Aunt Agni's stern voice. 'Your father wants you!' Aunt Agni did not even enter the room, but merely rapped imperiously on the door and went off, the sound of her feet like thunder on the tiled floor.

Serra felt shy as she entered the sitting-room. She had hastily dried her eyes on seeing the taxi, and of course she hadn't shed any tears since, but her face and eyes had by no means recovered and on seeing Dirk's expression she realized she must look a dreadful fright.

'What's wrong?' he asked before her father could speak.

'I thought you weren't coming.' She gave him a deprecating smile before adding inconsistently, 'But I knew you would, because you promised.'

He had certainly made an impression on her father, for he fairly beamed at Serra, saying she was a very lucky girl indeed, and he himself was fortunate in having his daughter marry into a family like Dirk's. All their relatives would be proud of her, and she must have a big wedding, he finally asserted, at which Dirk stepped in and explained that, as there was so little time, the wedding must be soon and, therefore, quiet.

'If that is your wish,' her father agreed, though he did add that all the relations would be disappointed, for in Greece a great deal of celebration attended a wedding.

They were married four days later and as neither Dirk nor Charles saw any reason why the small matter of Serra's entry into their lives should in any way interfere with their holiday plans they all went off to Beirut together, where they occupied three separate rooms at the fabulous St George's Hotel, reputed to be one of the most luxurious hotels in the whole of the Middle East. From her bedroom window Serra looked out on to the magnificent Bay of St George into which flowed the warm blue waters of the Mediterranean Sea. The luxury of her room took her breath away and on first entering she amused herself by switching everything on—the lights and air-conditioning and radio—and then she pressed a couple of bells, deciding not to do so again, for her action brought in a maid and a hotel porter.

'I'm sorry,' she said contritely. 'I was just trying everything.' Both gave her odd looks, shrugged their shoulders and departed.

The incident did not trouble her unduly and she hummed a little tune to herself as she unpacked her new clothes. These her father had insisted on buying for her, so pleased was he over the question of the dowry. There were some emotional repercussions when the time came for Dirk to take his bride away, but both Serra and her father felt much better when Dirk promised she could have a holiday with her father later on in the year.

'But you are not sending her alone?' Serra's father stared at Dirk owing to his phrasing, and, realizing at once that it would not be the thing to send Serra to Greece alone, Dirk promised that his sister would accompany her. It was Serra's turn to stare, for that was the first she had heard of a sister-in-law!

'Oh, but I am very happy!' Having finished her unpacking Serra sat down at the dressing-table and combed her hair. 'And I look happy!' Her eyes shone like stars; her cheeks were softly flushed. What a wonderful time she was about to have! Once she got to England she was determined to do everything, and although as yet she was rather vague about what constituted 'everything' Serra anticipated having a gay and carefree life.

On joining the two men half an hour later in the lounge she recounted the story about the bells she had pressed. Charles laughed; Dirk told her to control her impulses in future.

They went out into the sunny, sub-tropical city, a city teeming with noise and colour and animation. American cars swished past barefoot natives, their backs bent double under the loads they carried. There were domes and minarets, skyscrapers on the seafront; and inland, the masses of coral-coloured roofs of the little village houses. These houses were often set on ledges on the foothills of the limestone Lebanese Range, the mountains which backed and flanked the city. On these foothills grew the brilliant green umbrella pines and, in fewer numbers, the famous cedars of Lebanon. Behind the mountains was the desert, in front the sea swept away in a shimmering expanse of cobalt blue towards a horizon made indistinct by the heat haze quivering against it. On the waterfront streamlined yachts and steamers lay gracefully at anchor, flying international flags. Cargo boats were there, and brightly-painted schooners and brigantines which plied along the coast, loading and unloading on the way.

Serra was in a dream of sheer ecstasy. How had all this come about?—and in less than a week? Was she really married?—and to an Englishman, as she had always longed to be? Automatically she touched her wedding ring as if for proof that she really was a wife. In name only, granted, but that suited her fine. Dirk wanted to be free, and so did she. It was a wonderful arrangement for them both.

All along the street were pavement vendors, mainly selling fruit and vegetables. Even used as she was to masses of produce such as this Serra gasped at the fantastic variety and colour, piled in neat pyramids or mounds, or hanging from the trellis outside the shops. Smiling men invited them to buy while not showing any annoying persistence when either Dirk or Charles shook their heads.

'Aren't we buying any?' Serra looked up at Dirk, suddenly aware that she had no money, her three hundred drachmae having been spent with wild abandon on a pair of gloves to go with her wedding outfit, her father and Aunt Agni having overlooked this vital adjunct to her charming little suit of pale green linen.

'Do you want some?' Dirk frowned. 'You can't be carrying a bag of fruit about with you.'

'I'd eat it.'

'Not in the street, you wouldn't!'

She felt rather hurt by his tone and fell into a forlorn little silence. Aware of this, Charles presently tried to cheer her up by saying there would be all the fruit she could want on the dinner table that evening.

'It was just that I wanted to buy it, though,' she explained, bringing forth a smile without much difficulty. 'It's fun buying such things.'

'Fun?' Dirk looked down at her, his eyes puzzled. 'Is buying fruit your idea of fun?'

'You don't understand,' was all she said, and the matter was allowed to drop.

They returned to the hotel at seven o'clock and an hour later were dining on delicious Lebanese food and, as Charles had prophesied, a huge bowl of fresh local fruit was put before them.

During the meal the two men had been discussing a visit to a night club, and now, having decided on the Caves du Roy which stayed open till dawn, they spoke to each other in a way that made it patently clear that Serra was not to accompany them.

'Can't I come with you?' she ventured when the opportunity arose during a lapse in the conversation.

'You'd get too tired,' said Charles in a faintly apologetic tone. 'We'll be there for hours and hours.'

'I wouldn't get tired, I promise.' She looked at her husband. His face was set and unsmiling.

'You're too young for such places. As Charles says, we'll be there for several hours. No, you go to bed. It's half past nine, and I'm sure you're used to going to bed somewhere around this time?'

She nodded but went on to say,

'I'm on holiday, though.'

'All the more reason why you should go to bed. We've some busy sightseeing to do—starting tomorrow.'

From her bedroom window Serra watched them leave the hotel a few minutes later. She felt a little lost, and certainly not in the least tired. There was no reason why she shouldn't go downstairs and sit in the lounge, she thought, and, picking up a magazine Dirk had bought for her to read on the flight to Beirut, she went out and took the lift down to the lounge. Many celebrities sat around and Serra became so interested that she forgot her magazine, and it slipped off her knee on to the floor. A young man stooped and picked it up; Serra smiled as he placed it on the table, and thanked him. He gave her a smile in response and sat down opposite to her.

'You can't be here all alone?' His voice was pleasant, his eyes admiring. Serra felt shy, and an involuntary glance round was inevitable. Then she smiled at her action. No need for fear any more; she was no longer a timid, subjected little Greek girl. From now on she was English, possessing the right of freedom.

'Yes, I'm all alone.'

The young man frowned, misunderstanding her.

'Do you often travel about on your own?'

'I misled you,' she apologized. 'I'm here with my husband and a friend.'

'I see.' The young man glanced around. 'I'd better go, then,' he said, and stood up. Serra had an urge to keep him in conversation for a few moments, and then she would go to bed, she decided, even though she was still not in the least tired.

'You needn't go—not if you don't want to. My husband and his friend have gone off for the evening.' As soon as the words were out Serra realized her mistake. The young man stared at her in surprise, and no wonder, for she was very young, and very lovely.

'They've gone out without you?'

Serra was at a loss as to how she might repair the damage, but of course there was no way in which she could do so and all she said was,

'I don't mind. I quite like being on my own.'

He shook his head, still rather dazed.

'It isn't natural.' He looked her over with a swift all-embracing glance. 'You can't have been married very long?'

She did not answer that, but changed the subject, asking about various people who were sitting around. Obligingly he answered her questions, smiling at the 'oohs' which issued now and then from her lips as he mentioned a Greek millionaire or wealthy Eastern potentate.

'It's so exciting!' she exclaimed, turning an animated little face to take another look at the Greek millionaire. His yacht was in the bay, she knew, because Charles had pointed it out to her.

'Is this your first visit to the Lebanon?' her companion inquired, unable to take his eyes off her face.

She nodded.

'I'm from Greece,' she informed him.

'But you're not Greek, are you?'

'My father is, but Mother was English. My husband's English.'

He shook his head.

'I can't understand him going off and leaving you here all by yourself.' A small pause and then, 'Will you come dancing with me?'

Her pulse quickened. Dance ... she had been taught the Greek dances, so perhaps she would be able to follow the steps of other dances. To go dancing was undoubtedly an exciting prospect and she was tempted to accept the invitation. But as yet she was a little timid of spreading her wings. Newly uncaged, she faltered, afraid of the wide vista of freedom opening out before her; she longed to soar away, yet found that her wings were cramped from a long period of disuse.

'I don't think I can come with you,' she began when an English couple, having entered the lounge and taken a sweeping glance around, joined the young man, saying they were ready to go. Both looked oddly at Serra, then exchanged amused glances. Serra had the impression that her companion was in the habit of talking to strange girls.

'What's your name?' he asked.

'Serra.'

'Mine's Tom, and this is Clark and Maureen.'

Shyly she said,

'How do you do,' and began to finger her magazine with little nervous movements.

'Will you come now that we have a respectable married couple to accompany us?' invited Tom with an amused smile.

'I see he's been flirting with you,' put in Clark. 'Beware of such men as Tom!'

'Have you no one with you?' Maureen spoke, her eyes flickering with puzzlement as she noted Serra's wedding-ring, shining and obviously quite new. Tom hadn't even looked at the ring, let alone noticed its newness; it took a woman to do that.

'No, she hasn't; that's why I've asked her to come dancing with us.'

'You didn't tell me there were others,' Serra pointed out. 'I thought it was only you.'

'So you were afraid?' Tom laughed. 'No need to be. Well, are you joining us now that you know you're safe?'

'Yes, I'd very much like to join you.' She noted the strangeness in Maureen's eyes again and wondered if her slight accent had caused it. As they were in the taxi

37

on their way to a night club Maureen asked Serra where she came from.

'Greece.' Tom answered for her. 'But she's half English. And she's married to an Englishman.'

'Your husband's not with you?'

Serra bit her lip. She resented all these questions.

'My husband is with me, but tonight he's gone out with his friend,' she was forced to reply after a little silence.

A tiny gasp escaped Maureen, and her husband also expressed surprise by the quick turn of his head. However, the couple must have decided it would be bad manners to continue questioning her and they fell silent, leaving Serra to enjoy the lights and the bustling life going on all around her. Entering into a congestion of traffic, the taxi slowed down and then stopped. Two barefoot natives passed by carrying huge bunches of bananas on poles over their shoulders; along the pavements the fruit stalls were illuminated; neon lights flashed and flickered from high buildings, the dark outline of the mountains cut in undulating waves into the starlit eastern sky.

'I expect this sort of a scene is not by any means new to you?' Tom spoke at last, to Serra, who shook her head.

'It's rather like Greece, but different in many ways. Beirut's more Oriental than Athens.'

'Athens isn't Oriental at all,' said Clark. 'I always feel I could be in any city in the world——'

'No—oh, you couldn't! What about the Acropolis?'

'Take that away and you have a city—any city.'

'Except that you can't take it away,' she pointed out. 'When you think of Athens you automatically think of the Acropolis—no, you actually *see* it.' Her mind naturally wandered back to that day, less than a week ago, when she had met Dirk, and there had followed the momentous happenings which had resulted in her gaining her freedom, in her being able to go out like this and enter into the fun that would automatically have been at her disposal had her mother not married a Greek. She would have been brought up in England then, and used to the Western way of life. That was now opening out to her and although she was enjoying this visit to the Lebanon she couldn't wait to get to her mother's country. It was a green land, her mother used to say, with wild mountain scenery in the north, originally carved out of thousands of feet of volcanic rocks—the result of great volcanoes erupting masses and masses of lava—and a soft undulating landscape in the south. And it was in the south that Serra was going to live—in the beautiful county of Dorset.

The mention of a night club by Tom brought Serra back from her fanciful flight to England and she asked which night club they were visiting. It would not be quite the thing, she decided, for her to turn up at the Caves du Roy with these three people—not when her husband was there.

'Bacchus Caves,' Maureen told her. 'You'll thoroughly enjoy the atmosphere. The owner wanted it built underground and as work progressed a Roman wall came to light. This has been incorporated, forming one of the walls of the club. The idea of having the décor done in the Roman style resulted from the finding of the wall, and so you dance between massive columns.'

'It sounds fascinating!' Serra was relieved to know they were not visiting the same night club as Dirk and Charles; she felt she could not really have let herself go with her husband around—even though she treated the matter of her marriage lightly, scarcely feeling married at all.

The club was in semi-darkness, and all about were ancient relics from the Roman era. On the 'Celebrity Wall' were the names, just discernible in the muted light, of famous people who frequented the club. A table was found for them in a dim corner; they were served with drinks and a *mezé*, and presently Clark and Maureen got up to dance. Tom looked at Serra. She got up, deciding not to tell him she'd had no experience of these dances. Should she find herself unable to follow him then her admission could be made. To her surprise and delight she followed him like an expert, her cup of happiness quite flowing over when on returning to their table Tom remarked on her dancing to the others, who were already sitting down.

Clark then asked Serra to dance, and after that they sat drinking and smoking while the cabaret was on the floor. Serra felt so excited she could scarcely eat anything, but she drank all that was put before her and it was only when she suddenly realized her head was spinning in the most disturbing way that she came to the conclusion that she had taken rather too much.

That proved to be an under-estimation, as she soon discovered on getting up to dance again.

'You're tipsy!' Tom stopped on the edge of the floor and stared at her in some amusement. 'Aren't you used to it?'

'No—no, I'm not used to having so much. I just have an *ouzo* now and then at home.'

'Then why didn't you say? Your husband's going to be mad at you, I'm thinking.'

It was on the tip of Serra's tongue to tell Tom that her husband would never know anything about it because he had his room and she had hers. But fortunately she was not quite so tipsy as to forget that such a statement would invite a string of questions from the astounded lips of her companion.

'I'll have got over it long before we return to the hotel.'

'Better get you some black coffee.' Tom led her back to the table. Clark and Maureen had gone wandering off outside, saying they were too warm, and so Tom and Serra were alone.

The black coffee had arrived and Serra was sipping it, and sincerely wishing she had not taken so much wine, when Tom excused himself, saying he was going to wash his hands. Serra leant back against the soft upholstery of her chair. If she weren't so light-headed she would be feeling extraordinarily happy, she thought, taking another sip of her coffee. She would take care another time, though, for it wasn't very nice to be told she was tipsy—— Suddenly she blinked, closed her eyes and opened them again. Yes, she was actually seeing things now—for there was Dirk, accompanied by Charles and two ravishing blondes, being shown to a table not far from where Serra was sitting. 'Oh, dear, never again,' she decided firmly. Wine in moderation might be all right, but certainly not in the quantities in which she had been drinking it.

Slowly it began to dawn on Serra that she was not seeing things after all and she breathed a deep sigh of relief at the knowledge. Dirk was dancing with one of the blondes, who was looking up at him and fluttering her lashes. Charles was still at the table, talking in what appeared to be intimate fashion with the other girl. Suddenly Dirk stopped, right in the middle of the floor, and stared in disbelief at his wife. She smiled at him, but to her surprise received only a glower in return. Within seconds he had led his partner off the floor and was striding purposefully towards her.

'What the devil are *you* doing here?' he demanded wrathfully, and Serra blinked again.

'Hello—*y-yass ... oo*!' The words bubbled out, with a tiny explosion on the last syllable. Serra was too tipsy to remember that this greeting was never used at night. Dirk's face was like thunder. He asked again what she was doing here.

'Having—h-having f-fun,' she hiccuped. 'But wh-what are y-you doing here? You s-said you were g-going to the Caves—Caves—to the other cave!' Again there was a final explosion. Her head! If only it would not spin so! Out of the corner of her eye she saw Charles, his face a study of disbelief, approaching her table.

'I told you to go to bed!' thundered her husband. 'How did you get to this place?'

'In a taxi——'

'Serra, what are you doing here?' Charles's voice was more subdued, but stern nevertheless. Serra frowned at the two men in turn.

'Why are you both asking me all these questions?' she began in plaintive tones, when Dirk interrupted to say he had asked only one.

'No, you haven't. You've asked me two questions,' she corrected her husband in plaintive tones interrupted now and then by a return of her hiccups. 'And I've answered them both.' What was the matter with Dirk? she wondered. Anyone would think she had committed some sort of crime. 'You promised I could enjoy myself—that I could do exactly as I liked.' She directed a glance at Charles, invoking his corroboration of this statement. He moved uneasily, taken at a disadvantage.

'You did, Dirk,' he ventured at last, and he also received a glowering look.

'The girl's drunk,' declared Dirk, just as if he were not speaking of his wife at all.

'That's not a very nice word,' Serra complained, raising a quivering hand to her head, which was beginning to ache abominably. 'Tom was much more polite!'

'Tom!' Both men spoke together, though the exclamation was Dirk's alone.

'The nice young man who brought me. He's staying at our hotel. I was sitting in the lounge and he came and spoke to me.' Where was he? Serra looked around, but there was no sign of him.

'In the lounge?' exploded Dirk. 'You actually got up out of bed and came down after we had gone?'

'I wasn't in bed. I didn't want to go to bed so early, so I decided to sit in the lounge for a while.'

'You were actually picked up—in the hotel lounge!'

'Father said I picked you up,' she reflected mechanically—and irrelevantly. 'He said it was an English expression.'

'You shouldn't have come out with a strange man,' interposed Charles. 'Being Greek you should have known it was very wrong.'

'I'm not Greek. Besides, you're changing the subject. Dirk said I could please myself what I did, and so I came out——'

'Where is this Tom?' interrupted Dirk furiously. 'Why isn't he with you?'

'He went to wash his hands.' Serra glanced around again. 'There was nothing wrong in my coming out with him,' she added. The effects of the wine were inducing a belligerent attitude now and she frowned darkly at her husband. Charles intervened, trying to be helpful.

'Dirk has every right to be cross with you, Serra, for

although it might not be wrong for you to come out like this it is wrong of you to get soused....' His voice trailed away into silence as his friend sent him a murderous look.

'It was the wine,' explained Serra unnecessarily, concluding that the word Charles had used had the same meaning as drunk and tipsy. 'I liked the taste of it and took a little too much——'

'Get up,' ordered her husband, his face pale with suppressed fury. 'I said *get up*!'

'I don't think I can.' Serra's eyes wandered to the two blondes, sitting there, obviously endeavouring to fathom, from the distance, what this was all about. 'Don't leave your friends,' Serra said obligingly. 'I'll be all right in a little while. Tom will get me another cup of coffee——' She broke off, uttering a little squeal as her wrist was grasped and she was jerked to her feet.

'Did you have a wrap?' Dirk used soft icy tones now, but there was no doubt at all that he was in a blazing temper.

'No—but look here——'

'Then come on!' Dirk shot a furious glance at Charles. 'I'll have to take her back to the hotel. Keep those two occupied until I return!'

Charles was clearly troubled, and reluctant to leave Serra alone with Dirk.

'Perhaps you'd prefer me to take her back?' he offered tentatively. 'You could then stay with the girls.'

Dirk's eyes were like flint.

'I can't walk out on Tom,' Serra hastily put in before he could speak, and she added, 'But I must admit I feel dreadfully ill—rather like I felt that day I met you.'

'No, Serra!' Charles was horrified at what might happen. 'No, you mustn't—not here!'

Dirk still held Serra's wrist; he gave it a vicious jerk, just to relieve his feelings.

'Out,' he ordered, 'into the fresh air!' And as he literally dragged Serra along behind him she had no option but to obey. And by now she was feeling quite unable to argue further, not only because she too was afraid of what might happen, but also because she was feeling inordinately fearful of her husband. Through her befuddled brain she was aware of the commotion this was causing; everyone seemed to be enjoying the free entertainment, judging by their amused, interested faces.

Once outside, Serra was unceremoniously bundled into a taxi; Dirk got in beside her and rapped out an order to the driver. Charles, having followed them, was standing close to the taxi. As it drew away Dirk rasped through the window,

'And you said I wouldn't know I was married!'

CHAPTER THREE

As was to be expected Serra awoke the following morning with a searing pain in her head. Groaning, she sat up and reached for the water. Unrelieved by the drink, she lay down again, finding a cool place on the pillow for her head. But the throbbing was unbearable and she sat up again. Was that the time? Ten minutes past ten; everyone would have had their breakfast ... breakfast!

'Ugh,' she muttered, and slid out of bed. Well, at least her legs were stronger than when Dirk brought her in here last night—or rather, in the early hours of this morning. She was standing by the mirror when the door opened and her husband stormed in. So he was still in a temper. Serra could not for the life of her understand why, because he had promised not to interfere with her movements—and he really had no need to leave his girl-friend. Tom would have seen her back to the hotel, she felt sure.

'Well, miss, are you fully recovered?' Dirk spoke in rasping tones, which she deeply resented, full of self-pity as she was. And to call her miss like that! Her resentment grew with every second that passed.

'I feel awful,' she admitted in a sulky voice. 'My head's as big as a football.'

'And as empty. Had you no more sense than to carry on until you reached that disgusting state?' His dark eyes roved disdainfully over her; she reached for a négligé and put it on, a flush rising to her cheeks.

'It came on me all of a sudden,' she returned defensively. 'Naturally I'd have stopped if I'd known it was going to make me feel so ill.' Her voice broke a little and her eyes filled up. 'You're very unkind,' she accused on a tiny sob.

'Unkind! Do you realize you've shown me up! You were an absolute disgrace, and you'd better make up your mind to practise a little more decorum in future. I'm only thankful we weren't at home—for my people would be thoroughly shocked were they to witness such abandoned behaviour!'

'Are you saying I'm not good enough for your people?' Tears hung on her lashes and her lip quivered. All fight had gone out of her because of the way he regarded her and because of his cruel insinuation. 'You should have thought of that before you married me.'

'I heartily agree,' Dirk responded swiftly, and at that two great tears escaped on to her cheeks. 'I would remind you,' he continued icily, impervious to her tears—or so it seemed at the moment—'that you promised to be very good and—obliging is the word I seem to remember you using.'

She nodded, suddenly encompassed in guilt.

'Yes, I did promise to be those things.'

'And you were exceedingly grateful that I married you.'

She nodded again, unhappily.

'I'm still grateful—truly I am.' Perhaps he would divorce her, she thought, and send her back to her father. Then he would marry this Clarice whom both he and Charles had mentioned. 'I won't do it again,' she faltered, looking up at him appealingly. 'You see, with your saying I could enjoy myself I took it for granted I could go out and—and be free.' To her surprise his face softened and tiny lines of amusement appeared at the corners of his eyes.

'And is getting yourself tipsy your idea of enjoyment?' His eyes slid over her again; she pulled the négligé together and held it so that her scanty nightdress was completely covered.

'You know it isn't. I feel dreadfully ill even now.'

'I'll get you something,' he offered after a pause.

'Oh, thank you, Dirk. Will it cure this headache?'

He smiled reminiscently and she somehow knew that he himself had felt like this.

'Yes, it will cure your headache.'

'You're kind,' she said, forgetting that only a moment ago she had declared him to be the very opposite.

'Don't be misled,' he then warned. 'I'm overlooking it this time because you didn't know. But you know now—so make sure it doesn't occur again.'

It was lunch time before she joined Dirk and Charles, for Dirk had insisted on her remaining in bed for the rest of the morning. To her surprise she was able to eat her lunch, and in fact she made up for the breakfast she had missed. Charles looked hard at her several times but made no comment on what had occurred last night, nor did he even ask if she felt better. He was clearly relieved that no serious disruption had occurred between her and Dirk as a result of what had happened.

She remembered that they should all have gone off on a sightseeing trip, but was reluctant to bring the matter up, although she would have liked to apologize for being the cause of the necessary alteration in their plans. She meant to apologize to Tom and his friends, though and she said unthinkingly,

'Have you seen Tom this morning?'

'As I haven't the faintest idea who Tom is,' replied her husband drily, 'I'm unable to say whether I've seen him or not.'

She smiled deprecatingly.

'I forgot you hadn't met him—and of course you wouldn't know Clark and Maureen either.'

Both men looked interrogatingly at her.

'And who are they?' Dirk wanted to know.

'The other two. Four of us went out together.'

'Four? So you didn't go alone with Tom?' Charles gave a little satisfied sigh. 'There you are, Dirk. I knew Serra wouldn't do anything imprudent.'

'I was imprudent,' admitted Serra quickly, on realizing that some caustic remark was about to be uttered by Dirk.

'Why didn't you tell me last night that you'd gone out with these other two as well?'

'To tell you the truth, I forgot all about them.'

'That's understandable, I suppose,' her husband remarked smoothly.

Serra flushed and concentrated on peeling an apple.

'I'll have to apologize to them all,' she murmured as the silence continued.

'Yes, you should do that,' agreed Charles, adding that they must have been exceedingly worried at discovering she had vanished into thin air, as it must have seemed.

'No such thing,' argued Dirk. 'Someone would tell them what had happened.'

'They wouldn't know it was Serra's husband who had taken her out of the club, though.'

Taken? Dragged, was the word Charles should have used, decided Serra, her flush spreading as she saw Dirk's eyes light with amusement. Plainly he read her thoughts.

'Tom would guess it was my husband.'

'You told him you were married?' Dirk seemed surprised and she thought of the blonde he was with. *He* would not mention the fact of his marriage, she felt sure. How had he explained his action, though? Not that it mattered, for those were clearly good-time girls and as long as Dirk went back they would not worry too much about his private affairs.

'Certainly I told him I was married.'

'Then how did you explain the fact of your being alone?' Dirk sounded a little angry and she assumed a nonchalant manner.

'I told him I liked being alone.' Which was the truth, for she had used those very words.

'And yet you agreed to go out with him and his friends?'

She gave a tiny sigh, feeling she was being tied up in knots.

'I didn't really like being alone; I just said I did, so that Tom wouldn't think it strange that you had gone off without me.' She picked up a piece of apple and put it in her mouth.

Dirk allowed the matter to drop and a few minutes later they were all in their rooms, changing before going on to the beach, where it had been decided they would spend the afternoon.

That evening they dined at their own hotel, as on the previous evening, and afterwards Dirk and Charles went off on their own.

'Stay in your room,' warned Dirk, having taken Serra up himself. 'Read in bed, or something.'

She nodded, then stared at the closed door for a long while after he had gone. It would be different when they got to England, she told herself. She would make friends and be able to go out and enjoy herself. She stood by the window, looking out on to the lights and bustle of the city. Beirut had been called the 'Paris of the Orient' and she could see why, for although she had never been to Paris she had often seen it on the films. There was movement and gaiety and colour everywhere. The crowds were cosmopolitan; many languages were spoken there, among the carefree tourists who made up nine-tenths of the laughing, chattering throng.

At last Serra moved away, thinking of last night and wondering if, had she been more circumspect, Dirk would have let her go out again with Tom and his friends. She had seen them and apologized. They had regarded her oddly but retained their affability towards her. She felt sure they would have been only too pleased to have her with them again.

As there seemed no point in sitting on her bed, or in the chair, Serra got undressed and after taking a bath, slipped between the cool white sheets, where she lay, wide awake, thinking about Dirk and Charles and wondering if they had met the same two girls again or whether they had found two different ones. She fell to musing on whether Dirk and Charles danced all the time or whether they went off with their respective girls to find some secluded spot....

Was Dirk a rake? He had made no protest to the contrary when it was mentioned—when she, Serra had asserted she did not mind in the least if he were a rake. She gave a little sigh and turned over on her side. Putting out a hand, she snapped off the light. If only she had been brought up in England she would have married for love—and her husband would not have been a rake. 'But I must be grateful for having gained my freedom,' she said. 'Father always declared that it was sinful to desire what was out of reach.'

The following day they set out early in a hired car, making for Baalbeck. Dirk drove, with Charles sitting beside him and Serra in the back. Travelling along the famous Damascus highway, they spiralled up the precipitous slopes of the Lebanese mountains, glimpsing all the time the magnificent panorama of hill and plain and sea far below. The umbrella pines shone, brilliantly green under the fierce Eastern sun. They looked like huge mushrooms, and there seemed to be thousands and thousands of them. Serra sat happily gazing through the window, absorbing everything but talking seldom, for Dirk and Charles were all the time making conversation of their own, conversation which did not include her. They passed apple and apricot orchards, all arranged on immaculate terraces cut over countless years in the sides of the mountain.

After crossing Dahr-El-Baidar the vast upland Plain of Bekaa lay before them, hemmed in by the two flanking scarps of the Lebanon and Anti-Lebanon Ranges. The word Bekaa in Arabic meant 'depression', Dirk was saying over his shoulder, and the Bekaa Plain was a northern continuation of the Great Rift Valley of East Africa. It was a region of lush vegetation, being fed by two rivers coming down from the mountains protecting it.

Their first sight of Baalbeck, lying about midway between Jerusalem and Palmyra, came when they had almost spanned the plain, the columns of its mighty temples appearing between a screen of leafy poplar trees, rising like sentinels to a flawless Eastern sky.

Parking the car close to the acropolis on which the great Roman buildings stood, Dirk slid from his seat and, opening Serra's door for her, handed her out. It was the first little attention he had afforded her and although she had the impression that it was an automatic gesture she experienced a little thrill of pleasure and rewarded him with a swift and dazzling smile. His eyes flickered lazily over her face. He seemed to discover things he had not before troubled to notice and the little silence became tense. But Charles's voice broke into it as he told Dirk that he had locked the door at his side of the car. Dirk locked his own door and they all moved away on to the acropolis, the Greek name for any high city.

As with the more famous Acropolis of Athens, a propylaea led into the area where the temples were situated, the great Temple of Jupiter—the Roman equivalent of Zeus, king of all the Greek gods—had six massive columns left, that was all, but they were impressive in their incredible height, being the loftiest columns in the world.

'They seem to support the sky!' gasped Serra. 'Ours at Athens look like dwarfs to these!'

'Do I detect a note of jealousy?' Dirk asked in a teasing voice, and Serra laughed, a tinkling laugh like music echoing from a distant place.

'Ours is more famous—the most famous in all the world.'

'And it's older,' supported Charles, smiling at her.

'Yes, this is only Roman,' she said disparagingly.

'You *are* jealous of those columns.' Dirk threw her a perceptive look, cocking his head on one side in a small gesture that she found attractive. 'Those at Athens are less than half the height of these. The Romans obviously considered their Jupiter to be more exalted than your Zeus.'

'They were showy. And they copied all our styles of architecture. These columns are Corinthian.'

'You should be gratified that they—and many others remember—copied the Greek style. The greatest form of flattery is imitation.'

She nodded, tilting her head to look to the top of

the columns, which were surmounted by a fragment of frieze and cornice. The original gleaming crystalline limestone had weathered to a rich tawny-gold, while some of the other ruins had weathered with a slight difference, running through several shades of grey to fawn and a warm and attractive yellow-ochre. The other forty-eight of the original fifty-four columns in the Temple of Jupiter lay fragmented on the ground, demolished by earthquakes occurring sporadically over a long period of time. The second magnificent specimen of the Greco–Roman site of Baalbeck was the Temple of Bacchus, larger than the Parthenon at Athens but, in ancient times, called the 'little temple' because it was dwarfed by the enormous Temple of Jupiter, standing close but isolated from it.

'This is beautiful,' declared Serra, gazing at the temple in rapt admiration. 'It's so wonderfully preserved. I wonder how it's come to stand when others have been dashed down by earthquakes?'

'One of the mysteries of nature,' said Dirk seriously. 'It's so often the case—one thing stands while another falls.'

'This is said to be the finest Corinthian building of the entire Roman world,' Charles told them, perusing the guide book.

'Can we go up this staircase?' Serra was saying a few minutes later. They were inside the temple and Dirk nodded.

'Of course we can—let me go first; you can be in the middle.' It was a spiral stair, and Serra had never seen one of these in Greece.

'This is certainly magnificent.' They were above the temple now and from this new angle the roofless proportions of the interior appeared more beautiful than ever. They were viewed against the backcloth of a scarp on the Lebanese mountain, on which a vestige of snow still remaining glistened in the sun.

The sides of the temple were lavishly decorated with Corinthian ornaments—flowers and fruits, sheaves of wheat and vines. There was the god Pan, and Vulcan with his hammer; and Bacchus, the god of wine, covered with grapes. There was Diana the Huntress shooting an arrow; and Mars, the Roman god of war, clothed in armour. All these, and many more, were exquisitely carved in stone and could be seen clearly despite the fact that weather had resulted in the wearing away of most of the clear-cut outlines that must originally have enhanced the carvings.

'I always wonder how long these things took to do?' They were on ground level again and Serra was staring at the gate, although her words pertained to the whole magnificent complexity of the entire site.

'There were slaves, by their thousands. Remember, there were only two classes of Romans, the patricians and the plebeians, the latter being the slaves.'

'Not at this period.' Serra spoke firmly and with authority. Her husband looked at her in some amazement ... and with a certain amount of respect.

'Oh? Tell us some more.'

'These buildings date from a later period than that of which you speak, Dirk, a much later period—there's a gap of about four hundred years, in fact.' She was a different person, far removed from the timid little girl Dirk had met on the steps of the Parthenon only a week ago. She was assured and confident because she was fully conversant with her subject, having been interested in Greek and Roman history since she was very young. 'I admit there were numerous slaves, but the plebeians themselves were merely an inferior class who, eventually, obtained equality of status with the patricians.'

Dirk continued to stare at her, with growing respect despite the fact that he was piqued at the idea of being corrected by his wife. He had spoken without thinking, his interest being engaged mainly with the lovely carvings. The last thing he expected was to have his statement pulled to pieces in this authoritative manner.

'The plebeians were the descendants of captured people, though,' he said. 'They never did achieve equality in that they themselves were classed as patricians.'

She agreed with this.

'There was class distinction until the end, but the plebs themselves owned slaves.'

'I say,' intervened Charles at last, 'can either of you tell me what this is all about? Who the devil cares, anyway? These pats and plebs have been dead two thousand years.'

Serra laughed, but made no answer. Dirk said, in a faintly piqued tone,

'Serra evidently could not resist correcting my mistake,' and he added, 'You should listen, Charles, you would learn something.'

Serra looked uncertainly at her husband.

'Did I sound pompous——?' She wrinkled her brow. 'Is that the right word?'

'It is. And you did.'

She was not sure how to take him and she forced a shaky little laugh. To her surprise he responded to her laugh and said she must tell him some more later, because he was interested. He was sincere, she realized, and a sudden warmth entered into her. It was strange, but up till now she had not foreseen an occasion when she and Dirk would talk as equals. He appeared to her as someone a world apart, superior, disinterested in her as anything other than the object of use to which she had been put. When visualizing her life in England she saw herself as living a totally separate existence from that of her husband. He had stated he wished to carry on as if he were not married; he wanted no interference—that was why he had been reluctant to marry this Clarice, obviously. And so Serra had not visualized even entering into casual conversation with him. Perhaps she was attaching too much importance to the fact of his wanting her to tell him some more about the history of the people who had built this sanctuary, but she did not think so. It would be nice to talk with him sometimes, she thought, looking up at him as he stood by one of the columns, touching the stone with slender brown fingers. How handsome he was! Suddenly she felt he really was her husband—and a thrill of pride entered into her. Not many girls were possessed of a husband as good-looking and distinguished as hers.

'What are you thinking?' Charles wanted to know as he saw her glowing expression.

'It was nothing important,' she evaded, but involuntarily her eyes strayed to Dirk again. He had taken the guide book from Charles and was glancing at one of the illustrations, but he glanced up at Charles's words.

'You look as if you've come into a fortune,' he remarked, rather too casually, Serra thought, and lowered her eyes. For some incomprehensible reason she did not want her husband to read her expression.

'The Temple of Venus next,' he said, returning his attention to the guide book. 'It's over there.'

'It's always difficult to reconstruct, mentally, the ancient scene,' Serra was saying half an hour later as they were preparing to leave the site. 'There would be a grand stairway along which the procession would approach for the worship of the god—they always had this. Then a courtyard would be entered through a huge colonnaded portico And can you imagine all the magnificent statues, in gold and bronze and shining white marble? It must have been a most impressive scene.'

'And all for the worship of some heathen god,' put in Charles with a hint of disgust.

'You used to worship heathen gods,' she reminded him, but Charles would not have that.

'We never did!'

'Don't let us have an argument,' interrupted Dirk as Serra, with a little lift of her chin, opened her mouth to say something. 'It's time we were moving on.' They were including Damascus in the day's tour and now Charles took the wheel as they began to drive through the Anti-Lebanese chain of mountains. Contentedly Serra leant back, gazing around her and remembering that she was in the region of the world where Adam had lived, and in one of the valleys of the Anti-Lebanese mountains Abel had been slain. Baalbeck was believed by many people to be the oldest city in the world, having been founded by Cain as he sought for a haven where he could escape the curse of God. Later, Abraham lived in the city of Baalbeck for a considerable length of time.

With about half the distance covered they stopped for lunch, spending as little time as possible on it before resuming their journey to the ancient city of Damascus, one-time capital of an empire reaching from Spain practically to the borders of China.

'I'm lucky!' exclaimed Serra, clasping her hands in a little gesture of ecstasy. 'I never thought I'd see all this!' They were standing, shoeless, in the Great

Mosque of Omayad, one of the most magnificent mosques in the world. A guide was telling them of its former stupendous glory, when it had six hundred lamps suspended on golden chains from the high ceiling, when its walls were decorated with murals and mosaics of gold encrusted with precious gems. He indicated the shrine standing in the centre, telling them that here had reposed the head of John the Baptist. They listened, with other tourists, and when he stopped speaking Serra repeated her exclamation. Charles laughed and said,

'Better than being married to Phivos, eh?'

'Phivos! I would have had to sit at home and do my embroidery all my life!'

'No doubt you would have been engaged in other pursuits as well,' commented Dirk with a dry smile. His implication being evident, Serra blushed; Dirk's eyes wandering over her slender figure did nothing to help her get over her disconcertment. But she lingered over his words, seeing the dull life to which she would have been condemned, and with a frown she presently put it from her and dwelt on the pleasures to come.

There had been no opportunity, during her two brief days of marriage, of discovering much about the home that would be hers in England, but as they walked out into the great court of the mosque along with the other tourists following in the wake of the guide she found herself separated from Dirk. Charles was walking beside her and she seized this chance of questioning him about it.

'Dirk lives in a mansion, standing in magnificent grounds. Also in the grounds is the Dower House, where his mother and sister live. Jenny's always been close to Dirk—adores him, almost, and she wasn't at all pleased when it seemed he would marry Clarice.'

Charles stopped, and looked at Serra ruefully. 'Don't know if he'd be wanting me to talk like this to you, but you'll have to know what to expect, it's only fair.'

'Have you been his friend a long while?' They were different, she thought, with Charles opening and talkative, while Dirk was reserved—a deep thinker, she decided, and wondered, quite without reason, whether he would always be a rake. Some day, when he was older, he might not want to be gadding about with ravishing blondes, but might prefer to settle down and be a stay-at-home. That would be awful, she thought, frowning, for then he could just want her to settle down as well, and this she had no intention of doing. She was free at last and she meant to enjoy that freedom until she was very old.

'We've been friends a long while, yes. We went to school together—though Dirk is a little older than I, as you know.'

'Tell me some more about his house and his family.' She paused a second. 'I don't know much about the reason for his having to get married,' she ventured, sending him an uncertain glance from under her long dark lashes. They were walking very slowly along the colonnaded court and Serra was struck by the unbelievable glory of her surroundings. Yes, she was lucky! It was like a dream come true.

'His father was disgusted with his wild ways and left him his fortune only on condition that he married within six months of his death. The old man was told, a year ago, that he had only a few months to live.'

'So Dirk's father concluded that marriage would put an end to Dirk's—er—wild ways?'

'Marriage usually does,' grinned Charles ruefully, and added, 'That's why it doesn't attract me.'

'It was very clever of Dirk to think of marrying someone who would not interfere with his pleasures.'

Charles looked oddly at her, and then his glance strayed to Dirk, who was standing on the edge of the crowd clustered around the guide.

'It's to be hoped that you'll never come to resent his way of life,' he murmured, almost to himself.

'I'll never do that,' she rejoined confidently. 'I promised—and in any case, I want to live a life of freedom myself. This marriage suits me perfectly.' She paused. 'Is he very wicked?' she inquired naïvely, and Charles gave a loud laugh.

'You're cute, Serra. Yes, he is quite wicked.' And both to her own surprise and that of her companion Serra exclaimed,

'I don't believe you! I think he's only spirited!'

'Could it be that you prefer him only to be spirited, as you term it?' queried Charles strangely.

She paused in thought, looking towards her husband.

'Yes . . . yes, I do prefer him only to be spirited.' They were close to the others now and their steps became even slower. 'Tell me about his mother?' she invited, desirous of changing the trend of conversation. 'I expect she's a great lady?'

'You'll like her, Serra...' He tailed off thoughtfully and something made Serra ask,

'Will she like me, do you think?'

He seemed to give a little sigh, she thought, before he answered,

'I expect she will, when she gets to know you.'

Serra bit her lip. In the excitement of the past few days she had not given much thought to her husband's people. From a drab uneventful existence she had been swept into an exciting adventure where in the newness of her surroundings she could think of little else but her amazing good fortune. But now she was back on earth and she was conscious of some slight misgivings.

'She'll be horrified at her son's marrying someone unsuitable?' she murmured reluctantly, watching Charles's face closely as she awaited his reply.

'All mothers have their own ideas as to whom their children should marry. I expect she hoped he'd marry a society beauty—— You're a beauty,' he added with a smile, 'so she won't be disappointed on that score.'

Soft colour rose to Serra's cheeks at the flattery, but she was still troubled.

'Would she have liked Dirk to marry Clarice?'

A moment's frowning silence and then,

'No, I don't believe she would. You'll see Clarice when you get to England, and I think you'll agree with me that she's hard. Had Dirk married her,' he went on, 'it wouldn't have worked out at all because, as I said, she would have interfered in his life. Dirk didn't want to marry anyone, as you know, and this arrangement he has with you suits him fine. He'll have his freedom and that is all he cares about.' They had reached the others and as the guide had finished his discourse they left and went off on their own to look at the white marble tomb of Saladin, that fierce warrior who defeated Richard the Lionheart in the Third Crusade.

'Can we go to the Long Market?' Serra wanted to know when at last both Dirk and Charles declared they had done quite sufficient sightseeing for one day.

'You know about it?' Dirk was frowning slightly; she felt he did not want to go to the *souk* and her face fell.

'I've heard about it. You can buy beautiful things—very cheap, they are,' she added as an inducement even though she was quite sure Dirk wasn't in the least interested in obtaining a bargain.

'We have time,' observed Charles. 'Let the child have a delve into the market if she wants to.'

Dirk shrugged.

'Very well.'

'Have you got any money?' Charles asked the pointed question with his eyes on Dirk. Serra was given some money by her husband, who was thanked profusely by his grateful young wife.

'What are you intending to buy?' he inquired without much interest, and she told him she had no idea until she looked around.

She did not know how she came to be separated from Dirk and Charles, but she did, the crowds being dense, compounded both of natives and tourists. But, strangely, she was not too perturbed, feeling she must come upon them presently, so she gave herself up to the delights of the Arab market, situated against a background of ancient Roman relics. Traders in various and colourful costumes were gesticulating, and speaking in a language she could not understand; they were selling lovely brocades threaded with silver and gold, which Serra could not resist, although, having bought some, she did wonder what she would do with it. Then she bought a leather bag and some small souvenirs. The money Dirk had given her soon passed into the eager hands of the traders and it was not until she had completely spent up that she turned her attention to the problem of finding the two men in this maze of humanity. Her arms were full and she was hot and rather tired. She hoped she would run into Dirk and Charles soon because her purchases were becoming heavy. Perhaps she should not have bought the 'earthenware object', but the smiling Arab had assured her that it was very ancient, having been brought up out of the sea—and there was no doubt that it looked ancient, having little crusty things adhering to it, rather like barnacles. But what a weight it was ... and what did she mean to do with it, anyway?

'Where can they be?' An hour had passed, then another half hour, then another.... 'I'm lost,' she quivered. But scarcely had she uttered this despairing whisper than she heard her husband's voice and turned around, a cry of greeting on her lips. But it was never voiced.

'Where the devil have you been!' he thundered, oblivious of the tears that had fallen on to his wife's cheeks. 'Over two hours we've been searching for you!' He saw the pile of stuff in her arms and stared unbelievingly. 'You actually went shopping—instead of looking for us?'

'Dirk, old boy,' put in his friend soothingly, 'all's well that end's well. We've found Serra and that's all that matters.'

'I thought I'd easily find you,' she faltered, quite dismayed by her husband's scowling countenance. 'I've inconvenienced you and I'm very sorry.' She looked at Charles. 'Will you carry some of my things, please? My arms are aching dreadfully.'

A smothered curse issued from Dirk's lips.

'Throw the damned stuff away!' he ordered. 'Inconvenienced us, did you say? Do you realize we've a three-hour journey ahead of us—and it's already getting dark?'

'It was an accident,' she began, handing over some of her goods to Charles, who accepted them willingly, his good-natured face troubled and a little drawn. He had been anxious, that was clear, she realized, but even as she looked into his eyes she saw a sternness appear in them.

'You shouldn't have wasted time shopping,' he admonished, more to appease his friend than anything else. 'Not when you knew you had lost us.'

'If you're not very careful,' said Dirk awfully, 'I shall begin to wish I'd never set eyes on you!'

'Shall we get back to the car?' suggested Charles practically. 'There seems no point in standing here.'

Dirk gritted his teeth, but strode off without another word, followed closely by his wife and Charles.

Dirk drove in furious silence for mile after mile with neither of his companions venturing to break it. Now and then Charles would throw a half glance over his shoulder, but Serra was perched on the edge of the seat with her head down, wondering how she could have carried on so blithely, buying everything she saw and not even thinking there might be trouble in finding the two men. She supposed she had not been much more than a quarter of an hour in getting rid of her money; for the rest of the time she had been wandering around, becoming more and more frightened as the minutes and hours passed. Two hours ... it had seemed like two days. And all Dirk could do was be angry with her. He could have shown a little sympathy. Now if it had been Charles he would have been so relieved he would have said nothing—or if he had it would have been something kind.

They had to rush into dinner, and still Dirk was looking like thunder. Charles tried to open a conversation but was answered in monosyllables, and Serra felt sure Dirk was already regretting having married her.

'I'm very sorry,' she said in a small voice when the meal was almost over. 'I won't do anything like that again.'

'You never said a truer word! You won't get the chance!'

'You mean you won't ever give me money again?' The idea appalled her. She had had a vague idea that Dirk would make her a huge allowance. 'I wouldn't spend it like that another time.'

A glowering glance and then,

'What a holiday! I'll remember this place, and no mistake!'

'I'm beginning to think,' interposed his friend mildly, 'that, having married Serra, you'll now have to develop a sense of humour.'

She sent him a speaking look. This was no time for frivolities, it said. But to her surprise her husband returned, in tones that had lost much of their wrathful edge,

'I believe you're right, Charles.'

Serra instantly threw off her haunted look.

'Am I forgiven?' she asked, her voice also brightening.

'Unless the rest of the holiday's to be spoiled,' he said, 'I've no option but to forgive you.' He gave a small sigh before adding, 'You'll have to mend your ways, though—and before we get home.'

CHAPTER FOUR

CHALCOMBE GRANGE was approached by a mile-long avenue of ancient oak trees, and backed by a massive park. Standing on a rise above the lovely Dorset village of Portford Magna, it could be seen for miles around, its impressive Palladian south front facing the sea.

Having said goodbye to Charles at the airport, Dirk and his new wife drove by car to his home. As they proceeded along the drive Serra several times gave little gasps of disbelief.

'England's wonderful!' she breathed, clasping her hands tightly in her lap as if by this gesture she would soothe the wild beating of her heart.

'My home isn't England,' Dirk laughed.

'I like everything I've seen up till now.' She had been enthralled all the way from the airport, looking this way and that, afraid of missing something. 'It's so green everywhere.' Her fascinated gaze was on the house, and instead of her heartbeats becoming calmer they were racing now as the car was coming to a halt on the wide imposing forecourt.

'Dirk ... I'm frightened,' she quivered, turning to him as he switched off the engine.

'Rubbish. I've told you, my mother won't be seeing you until I've had a talk with her.'

'But—but she'll be so surprised that you're married.'

'Certainly she will, but she knows I was looking for a wife. It's just a little sudden, that's all.'

He seemed so calm. Serra gave a deep sigh. If only she could be equally calm! But it would soon be over—the first meeting—and then everything would be all right, she tried to assure herself.

On alighting from the car she stood looking up.

'You've been copying our architecture too,' she said rather accusingly. 'But your Doric columns are debased.'

'So I believe.' Dirk closed the car doors. 'Everyone who was anyone copied Greek architecture during the Renaissance period. Come, you can't stand there all day finding fault with the building.'

'Oh, I wasn't!' He was striding towards the massive arched front door and she tripped along after him. The door swung inwards as if he had sent a radar signal to the butler.

'You're back, sir. I trust you had a pleasant holiday?' Dirk was already in the hall; a final little run brought Serra to his side. The butler, stout round the middle and so distinguished with his haughty features and greying hair that he could have been the master of the house rather than Dirk, looked questioningly at his employer.

'Meet my wife, Preston.' Dirk spoke casually, just as if he were remarking on the weather. 'Is my mother over at her own place?'

'Yes, sir.' The question following on the introduction afforded Preston time to recover from his surprise. Of course, he would know about the will, thought Serra, and that was why he wasn't evincing the astonishment she had anticipated. 'How do you do, madam. Welcome to your new home.' Covertly he looked her over; a pained expression settled on his aristocratic features.

'Thank you, Mr Preston.' She tried to disarm him with a smile but failed, little knowing that her prefixing of his name had lowered her still further in his estimation.

Dirk was walking away and she followed, staring about her and allowing her lips to form recurrent 'ohs' while keeping one eye on Dirk, lest she should lose him in this vast edifice. She was walking on thick carpet; the walls of the great hall were covered with tapestries and oil paintings and swords and chain-mail jackets. The ceiling had been painted by Verrio and Serra gasped at the intricacies of flower patterns and clouds, of birds and animals and cherubs with outspread wings. Before her was a wide staircase curving out at the top to form a semi-circular gallery. All the way along its walls portraits were hung—portraits of Dirk's ancestors, she concluded.

Dirk opened a door, threw a look over his shoulder to make sure she was following and entered the Green Drawing Room.

Serra stopped at the door; this wasn't her world. This was some exalted paradise to which she could never belong. Fear took possession of her and she lifted appealing eyes to her husband's face. He regarded her from the centre of the room, and perhaps it was because she looked so small, standing there in the great oak doorway, with its exquisite carvings and Ionic-style pillars, that he smiled reassuringly and held out his hand to her. She moved then, and forced a smile as she put her cold hand into his and felt its warmth and its strength and its support as Dirk curled his fingers round hers.

'You're not afraid?' His eyes were kind, and quizzical. She saw again those little fan lines spreading to his temples and remembered her swift assertion that Dirk was not wicked—only spirited, she had told Charles, and she now knew that her words had reflected a desire, deep and fervent.

'I'm not afraid now. It was just butterflies——'

'Lord—no!' He examined her face for some sign of a green tinge that might have appeared.

She laughed, a little shakily, perhaps, but she was no longer nervous.

'Not that kind of butterfly!'

'Thank heaven. I don't want you looking like a washed-out rag when I bring my mother over to meet you.' Releasing her hand, he told her to sit down. 'Why didn't Preston take your coat?' he frowned, suddenly realizing she had it draped over her shoulders like a cape.

She laughed again.

'Mr Preston was too shocked to ask for it.'

'You don't say Mr Preston—just Preston.'

'That doesn't sound very polite; he's old enough to be my grandfather.'

'Not quite. Preston in future. Remember. Now, sit down,' he said again, indicating a small tub chair delightfully upholstered in quilted crimson satin. Serra obeyed and Dirk told her how she must behave, and what she must and must not do. He knew Charles had enlightened her on certain matters, but now he told her a little more. He had business interests in London and was forced to go there periodically. Serra wondered if it were solely business that took him to the capital but naturally refrained from questioning him. That he would have these absences pleased her no end, for it meant that, should she get into any scrapes, her husband would never come to hear about them. He also told her that his sister, Jenny, might at first appear not to like her, but Serra must take no notice. Jenny did not live at the Grange, so Serra would not come into regular contact with her. The Dower House was away at the far side of the park, Dirk told his wife. 'Now,' he said finally, 'I'll ring for a maid who'll take you up to your room. Tidy yourself up and put on another dress. You'll have to do everything yourself for a little while, just until I get a maid for you.'

'A maid?' Her eyes opened wide. Her mother had told her about English ladies having maids, but.... 'I don't want a maid, Dirk. It's not necessary——'

'Certainly it's necessary. Don't interfere in things you don't understand.' He pulled a bell-rope and Preston appeared. Serra looked at him, trying to read his expression. It was impassive, but she sensed the pain behind the mask. Preston definitely did not approve of her.

'Send Janet in here.' Curt tones. Had Dirk also noticed the hidden disapproval in his butler's wooden countenance?

'Certainly, sir.'

Janet was a Scot with clear grey eyes and ruddy cheeks. Unlike Preston she was quite unable to conceal her surprise and she gave Serra an incredulous glance when Dirk said,

'Janet, will you take my wife up to the blue bedroom?'

'Y-your w-wife, sir?'

'And see that the suitcases are taken up. Mrs Morgan's are in the back of the car; mine are in the boot.'

'Yes, sir.' Even then she seemed unable to accept the evidence of her ears and it was only when Dirk asked what she was waiting for that she emerged from her stupor and took Serra up to the room next to Dirk's. In a little while Serra heard him moving about and knocked at the dividing door.

'Come in.'

She entered, glancing round. The walls were covered with gold wallpaper, to match the elaborately-gilded ceiling, from which hung two enormous cut-glass chandeliers. Two beautiful commodes decorated with gold leaf stood one at either side of the John de Val fireplace above which was an enormous gilt-framed mirror. The room, she realized, was very similar to her own, differing in colour and having a view to the soft, undulating chalk hills, whereas Serra's room looked south, on to the sea.

'You didn't tell me what to do when I'm ready,' she began as Dirk waited, not very patiently, for her to finish her examination of the room.

'Wait in your bedroom—— No, go down to the Blue Drawing Room and wait there. I'll bring Mother over in about half an hour.'

'The Blue Drawing Room?'

'When you're ready ring for Janet; she'll show you where it is.'

She twisted her hands.

'Won't you take me down?'

'I'm going over to the Dower House immediately, so I won't be here.' He picked up a hairbrush; it was a sign of dismissal and she turned into her own room, automatically looking round for the bell. A hefty rope of twisted silk thread hung by the blue-draped tester bed and she supposed that was it.

A dream of a bathroom led off her bedroom and she took a shower, then she dressed carefully, but wished she could press her dress, for it was creased from being folded in her suitcase. However, she thought she looked quite presentable when, twenty-five minutes later, she summoned up sufficient courage to tug at the bell-rope.

Janet appeared and Serra, trying desperately to sound composed, asked to be taken down to the Blue Drawing Room.

Its magnificence surpassed even that of the great hall and she stood in the middle of the room, gazing first at the lofty ceiling, decorated in white and gold, and then at the walls with their array of paintings by Van Dyck and Turner and many other notable artists. There was Chippendale furniture and French marquetry and Chinese porcelain of the like Serra had never even imagined, let alone seen. She thought of her father's villa, with its tiled floors and distempered walls and paucity of furniture.

'Well,' she said with an effort at her innate buoyancy, 'I'll have to get used to it, seeing that I'm here to stay.' She walked about, touching this and that—and it was when she touched a panel in the wall that she uttered a little cry and leapt back. A secret door.... She had heard of such things and after the initial shock she stepped into the aperture. Was it a priesthole? she wondered, shivering a little because it smelled musty and a cobweb touched her cheek. Then she heard voices—coming from the next room, she surmised, putting her ear to the wall.

'But what about Clarice?' the voice was musical and Serra thought she would have liked it had it not been edged with angry protest.

'To the devil with Clarice! I never asked her to marry me.'

'She must be taking it for granted that you will marry her, though——'

'I am married.' Impatient the interruption from Dirk.

'Everyone expected you to marry her.'

'Then everyone will be disappointed. I'm not tying myself up with a family like that. Serra won't expect any fuss and attention—she hasn't been brought up to the idea that her husband must be around all the time.'

'You're quite mad, Dirk, I always knew it—but it was your father. I did hope you wouldn't take after him. I had a dreadful time with him.' A pause. Serra pressed closer to the thin wood panelling. 'This girl sounds an oddity——'

'She isn't an oddity; she's perfectly normal.'

'Normal?' echoed the musical voice with satire. 'You call it normal to marry a complete stranger?—and to be quite content to let him carry on as if he were still single?'

'I've explained the whole situation leading up to our marriage,' impatiently from Dirk. 'In her country the women are not considered. They just do as they're told. I've been very fortunate in finding her.'

A small silence and then, in a voice of resignation,

'Well, what's done is done. She's in the next room, you say? Then let us go. I'm exceedingly interested in meeting this paragon of wifely submission—— What on earth's that?'

The door had slammed to on Serra, bringing down a great cloud of dust and cobwebs. She let out a scream and began hammering on the panel.

'Let me out!' She was terrified, imagining herself dying, slowly, from lack of air and food. 'Let me out!' She stopped on hearing voices coming from the drawing-room. The panel slid open and she sagged with relief.

'Serra—what——?' Dirk stood there, with his mother, immaculate and poised, her face a study of incredulity as Serra, her ashen face covered by dust and grime, made a rapid escape from her prison.

'Normal, did you say?' murmured Dirk's mother, looking up at him.

'Your manners!' he snapped. 'Serra, what do you

mean by going in there!' He was uncomfortable, but trying to retain his composure. Serra was too relieved at escaping an early death to trouble her head about her unceremonious first encounter with her mother-in-law.

'The—the door shut on m-me.'

Her husband drew an exasperated breath.

'Why didn't you sit still! Prowling about like this. You'd better go and do something with yourself!' He looked as if he would dearly have liked to shake her, she thought, although he still endeavoured to retain some semblance of calm.

'Aren't you going to introduce me?' inquired his mother softly, her eyes taking in every detail of Serra's appearance.

Dirk glared at her, his face colouring slightly under its tan.

'Don't be frivolous! Serra—do as I say!'

'Yes——'

'The servants,' interrupted Mrs Morgan, slanting a look in her son's direction.

'Lord, yes.' He gave his wife a glance fit to kill her. 'Someone will see you if you go upstairs. What made you go in there?'

'I touched a panel,' she began unhappily, as the full import of her action struck her. Dirk had wanted her to make a good impression on his mother—just to mitigate the shock, as it were. Serra herself had desired to make a good impression, but now she realized she must be an object of ridicule to the elegant woman standing there, her expression now one of amusement rather than surprise. 'And then—then I heard voices——' She broke off, touching her mouth with a quivering hand as she saw what her admission meant.

'You listened to our conversation?' Dirk's voice was

dangerously quiet, his eyes like flint. 'Is that why you stayed inside?'

She nodded and hung her head. What must his mother think of her?

But to her surprise Mrs Morgan seemed to consider the farce should be terminated and said practically,

'I'll see if the coast is clear. I'll give a little whistle if it is and then she can come up.' She went out and for a few awful seconds Serra was alone with her husband.

'I'm sorry,' she began when he interrupted her.

'You'll be more than sorry if you continue like this, my girl!' Coming very close, he wagged a furious finger in her face. 'I'm just about reaching the end of my patience!'

'Perhaps,' she faltered, 'you'd have been better with Clarice.'

'There's no perhaps about it,' he retorted brutally. 'I *would* have been better with Clarice!'

Serra could think of nothing to say to that, and in any case Mrs Morgan was letting out a low whistle and, taking Serra by the arm, Dirk propelled her to the door and gave her a final shove which took her into the hall. His mother was at the top of the stairs.

'Quickly,' she beckoned, and Serra ran up the wide stairway and into the privacy of her room. Mrs Morgan closed the door on her and went away.

After washing and changing Serra stood a long time by the dressing-table, most reluctant to go downstairs again. But she would have to do so and at last she went to join her husband and his mother. Serra wondered at once what had been said in her absence, for Dirk appeared to be mollified and his mother actually smiled as she invited Serra to sit down. She's sorry for me, Serra concluded, taking possession of the chair and sending a sidelong glance at Dirk.

'As the introductions have been made we might as well have tea.' Mrs Morgan suggested. 'And then we can talk over it.'

'I heard you say I was an oddity,' Serra murmured in an apologetic tone, 'and now, I suppose, you are convinced of it.'

'If you eavesdrop,' said Dirk, 'and eavesdropping appears to be a favourite pastime of yours—then you must be prepared to hear unflattering comments about yourself.' He sat down after having rung the bell.

'Don't be so heartless, Dirk,' admonished his mother, smiling as she was rewarded with a grateful glance from her daughter-in-law. 'I'm sorry, dear, that I said that, because you're not an oddity at all. In fact, I'm sure you and I shall get along fine together.'

Yes, Mrs Morgan was sorry for her. Serra frowned at the idea because she did not want pity. Dirk was regarding his mother curiously, her words appearing to surprise him.

'I sincerely hope we will.' Serra glanced towards the door as it opened and Janet stood there.

'We'll have tea, Janet, please.'

'Yes, sir.' The girl's eyes flickered from Dirk to his mother, as if she would discover what was going on.

'Tell me about yourself,' invited Mrs Morgan when the door had closed behind the maid. 'What part of Greece do you come from?'

'Athens—well, just outside.'

'Your mother came from England, Dirk tells me. What part?'

'The Midlands, but I don't know where that is.'

'You have no relatives here?'

'I might have, but they'll be very distant ones.' She met her mother-in-law's gaze, her eyes wide and faintly unhappy. 'Mother never mentioned any cousins, or anything.'

A tiny sigh came from Dirk. He looked immeasurably bored, and Serra felt he would rather be anywhere but here, with his wife and his mother.

'You're going to find our way of life a little strange at first,' Mrs Morgan was saying. 'But you'll soon get used to it. My daughter will take you under her wing and you'll soon make friends.'

A brighter expression spread over Serra's lovely face.

'How old is Jenny?' she inquired, and Mrs Morgan gave a little start.

'Has Dirk not told you all about us?' Automatically Serra shook her head; Mrs Morgan looked at her son and murmured admonishingly, 'That was remiss of you.'

'We haven't had much opportunity of talking together,' Serra told her hastily in defence of her husband. 'You see, Charles was there. He did tell me a little about you, and this house, and he said Dirk had a sister called Jenny.' She stopped, wondering why Dirk was glowering at her. But his mother laughed.

'What a priceless situation! Dirk, you've done some mad things in your life, but this is just about the limit. Why did you allow him to persuade you, child? Surely you could have done better for yourself.

'Better?' Serra's big eyes became wide and incredulous. 'I must be the luckiest girl on earth!'

A dry look now from her mother-in-law.

'Talking of persuasion,' intervened Dirk before his mother could return an answer to that, 'if Serra is honest she'll admit that it was *she* who persuaded *me*.'

Absently his wife nodded.

'I did—it was because I wanted to be free.'

'Free?'

'Like English girls. Dirk promised I could do as I

liked. We both thought it was a good arrangement——' She threw a doubtful glance at her husband. 'But now—now I'm very much afraid you're regretting it?' Her eyes appealed, urging him to deny this, and in spite of himself Dirk had to laugh.

'Not yet—not quite. But if you get into one more scrape then I shall regret it.'

'Scrape?' Mrs Morgan was interested; her blue eyes twinkled and it would seem she was thoroughly enjoying this little scene.

'I got drunk,' blurted out Serra, incurably honest.

'You——?'

'Only because she's not used to having a drink,' put in Dirk hastily, suddenly stern again. 'Do you have to confess everything?' he demanded. 'You seem quite determined to shock my mother.'

'My dear Dirk,' said his mother drily, 'you yourself have long since made me immune to shocks.' She turned to Serra. 'Tell me all about it? How did you come to get drunk?'

After an uncertain glance at Dirk Serra obliged, amazed at the equanimity with which her narrative was received. Even Dirk had lost his ill-humour, it seemed, for he too was regarding her in some amusement.

'I presume,' commented Mrs Morgan presently, 'that this was not the only scrape you got into—not by the way Dirk spoke, that is?'

'There was the market,' Serra told her. 'I lost Dirk and Charles and they were searching for me for two hours. Dirk was not very pleased about it.'

'That's understandable.' Mrs Morgan looked at her son, seeming to be seeing him through different eyes. 'Do I recall your saying, a short while ago when you came over to the Dower House, that you wouldn't even know you were married?' He made no answer and she continued, 'Tell me more about the market, Serra?'

A little shamefacedly Serra mentioned her purchases, whereupon Dirk interrupted to say,

'Those Arabs saw her coming. Such a conglomeration of rubbish I have never before seen, nor do I ever wish to see again. I made her leave it in the hotel bedroom.'

Serra's face creased into a reluctant smile.

'I'd never had so much money to spend, you see.'

The tea was brought in and they had it on a small table by the window. The sun was bright, shining on the lawn and fountain and on the distant hills. Mrs Morgan asked more questions—about Serra's home and her father and even about the boy she should have married, for Dirk had mentioned this in his initial explanation to his mother. Serra spoke, openly and naïvely, her heart lightening all the while. Mrs Morgan was nice, and that was such a relief. Serra only hoped Jenny would be just as amicable as her mother, although Serra had not forgotten Dirk's warning that, at first, Jenny might not appear to like her. And this, she supposed, was because Jenny was very close to her brother—so Charles had said—and she would probably not care for the idea of Dirk's marrying someone from abroad.

Jenny had been out at the time Dirk went over to the Dower House, but she arrived home later and, being told the news by her mother, who had left the Grange immediately after tea, she promptly got into her car and drove through the park to her brother's home.

Dirk had been showing his wife round the house, but all the while she had the impression that he was inordinately bored with his task. Serra went about with him, wide-eyed and wondering how anyone could need so many rooms. There was the Yellow Drawing Room and the Green Saloon and the China Room and the Sculpture Gallery and numerous others.

'Don't you have anywhere to sit?' she murmured, revealing her decision that all was far too vast and treasure-filled for real comfort.

'Sit?' They were in the breakfast room and Serra was eyeing the silver on the sideboard. 'I hadn't noticed we were short of chairs.'

She laughed a little deprecatingly.

'I meant—haven't you a cosy room—you know, all crumpled-cushiony and dented chairs and spilling logs. I've seen rooms like that on the English films we used to have.'

His eyes lit with amusement.

'You want to slum it at times, I take it? Yes, we do have such an apartment.

It was situated on the south front of the Grange, overlooking the soft wooded slopes of Cranbourne Chase with, closer to, the lush vegetation of the parkland surrounding the Grange. Yet despite its obvious comforts—with its big couch and enormous easy chairs, and its scattered rugs and wide stone fireplace —it still possessed the same air of luxury as the rest of the house. Here was ease, yet dignity, comfort, yet detachment.

'I like it very much.' Serra breathed a tiny sigh of satisfaction as she stood and looked around. Then she lifted her face and met her husband's gaze, which she had sensed had been fixed on her since the moment of entering this lovely graceful apartment. 'You have a very beautiful house, Dirk, and I don't know how I come to be here in it.' She shook her head; the shining hair sprang with life and freshness on to her cheeks and then settled, a glorious crown for the classical face of a beautiful Greek *kore*. 'It's a dream and a miracle, and I keep thinking I'll wake up and find myself married to Phivos.'

To her surprise he frowned darkly at this and she slid her head sideways; an interrogating gesture but one that was inordinately attractive too, and a strange expression crossed her husband's face before he said, with quite unnecessary abruptness, she thought,

'You must forget Phivos. This is your life from now on.'

A small hesitation and then,

'You're not sorry you married me, are you, Dirk?'

Surprising her again, he ruffled her hair in a playful gesture.

'I've said not yet. I've also threatened I would be sorry if you didn't keep out of scrapes. What made you go into that chimney?'

'Was it a chimney? I thought it was a priest hole.'

'It would have been some sort of hiding-place at one time or another, but it's also part of the chimney.' His lips curved in amusement. 'What a sight you looked! Good thing you weren't seen by any of the servants; they'd have talked about it until you were ninety.'

She had gone red, but at that moment a maid came into the room to say Dirk's sister was in the drawing-room.

Serra cast a rather frightened glance at her husband.

'Will your mother have told her of my—my escapade?'

He shook his head.

'Most unlikely.' A pause and a smile as they both turned to leave the room which Serra knew she would use more than any other in the house. 'You've made a hit with my mother. I congratulate you, for she had high hopes of marrying me off to some wealthy heiress.'

'She's nice.' They were passing through the hall, making for the high oaken door leading into the room where Serra had first met her mother-in-law in such humiliating circumstances only a few hours earlier.

'I agree. Mother and I understand one another and, consequently, we agree about most things. She's resigned to you, as I knew she would be without much delay.'

'Charles told me you were very close to your sister,' she began, her heart thumping as they drew nearer to the enormous door behind which her sister-in-law was waiting. 'Is that why she might not like me?'

'We are close—though heaven knows why. Jenny's disapproval of my wicked ways has been evident since the moment she was old enough to know exactly what they meant.' He opened the door and a second later Serra was shaking hands with Jenny, whose blue eyes, piercing like those of her mother, took in every detail of the flawless features before moving almost imperceptibly over Serra's whole figure.

'How do you do, Serra.' The handclasp was firm, but the eyes which were now raised to her brother's face held an expression reminiscent of that which Serra had sensed lay behind that of Preston on being introduced to her. Pain ... and faint disbelief. Faint...? Jenny knew her brother had to marry and, like her mother, she would also know that he was quite capable of acting in an unorthodox manner; this was the reason for the absence of any real surprise. Of course, she would already have received all the details from her mother, so in any case she was forewarned, knowing just what to expect. 'I hope you like your new home?' Sarcasm— which, besides making Serra blush, also brought a sparkle to her eyes.

'I like it very much. It is in great contrast to my home in Greece,' and she added slowly but with emphasis, 'It's more like the buildings of our past—noble and elegant like the temples one sees in Greece. But here Dirk has many treasures, in addition.'

Dirk frowned darkly at her, saying plainly that there was no need to be rude to his sister. Jenny went a trifle red, and withdrew her hand from Serra's.

'You have a bite. I always believed Greek girls were meek and subdued, with very little to say.'

'But I am not a Greek girl. My mother was English, and in any case, I am now married to an Englishman.'

'You sound as though you'd rather be English than Greek?'

'I quite like the mixture,' returned Serra, surprising both her husband and his sister. 'But I have always longed for the freedom of my mother's people. As you say, Greek girls are meek—which is inevitable, seeing that they've occupied an inferior position for more than three thousand years. I suppose my mother's genes must have been dominant in me, because I've never been satisfied with my position of inferiority.'

Both Dirk and Jenny had been smiling as Serra talked and now they both laughed, Dirk with humour, Jenny with a sort of deprecating satire.

'Shall we sit down?' Dirk indicated a chair and Serra took possession of it. His sister sat on the couch, leaning back and crossing her legs one over the other and looking at her new sister-in-law through half closed eyes. 'A drink, Jenny?' She nodded and he handed her one; his eyes met Serra's, a twinkle in their depths. 'Lemonade?' he asked without much expression.

She flushed but her chin tilted. However, before she had time to ask for the sherry which she wanted a glass of lemonade was handed to her and rather than cause a small scene she accepted it, fully aware of Jenny's amusement. A little girl from an Eastern country, they thought her, a girl without any strength of character, a girl who had known her place for years and who would continue to know it. Well, Jenny at least would get a surprise, for Serra meant to take her husband's promise seriously and do exactly as she liked. Just give her time to feel her feet, and she would show Jenny that she wasn't at all meek. In fact, Serra fully hoped that in a few weeks' time she would possess a poise and self-assurance matching anything her sister-in-law could produce.

'She didn't like me, as you said,' commented Serra when Jenny had made her departure half an hour later.

'It's only temporary,' responded Dirk without much interest. 'I'm a sort of idol to her—though heaven knows why—and she's probably been thinking I'd marry someone more suit——' He broke off, but his eyes kindled with amusement. 'You know what I mean?'

She nodded and said she hoped that in time Jenny would accept her and be friendly.

'Your mother promised Jenny would take me under her wing,' she ended on a tiny sigh. How was she to get around without someone to assist her?

'She will—eventually. You'll have to be patient, but it'll all work out right in the end.' He paused a moment, looking rather appreciatively at his wife. 'You know, Serra, you're quite refreshing. There was no indignation just now when I inadvertently mentioned someone more suitable. You're just the wife for me, and as you overheard me telling my mother, I was exceedingly fortunate in finding you.'

She smiled rosily at him.

'Thank you, Dirk.' And she decided to add, 'I'll not get into any more scrapes, I promise.'

'I'm relieved to hear it. As I've said, I don't want to feel I'm married, not in any way whatsoever.'

'You won't, Dirk. You must do just as you like—act in the way you've been used to all this time.'

'I intend to, my child.'

'And I shall be free too.' A small silence; she sent him a hesitant glance from under her long dark lashes. 'Will I have—have some money?'

'Of course. Once a month you'll have a cheque paid into your bank——'

'I haven't a bank.'

'Don't interrupt. You will have a bank—and, as I've said, you'll have a cheque paid into it monthly. Now——' he wagged a forefinger at her—'don't go mad like you did at the *souk* in Damascus. The money's to last you a month, so you'd better have some system as regards your spending.'

'Is this money for my clothes as well?'

'No—you'll have an account at the shops—I haven't any idea about such things,' he added with a hint of impatience. 'Jenny will tell you all about it.'

She felt lighthearted and glowing with excitement and anticipation.

'So I can have beautiful clothes?'

'Certainly.' His eyes slid over her dress; it was of plain grey wool and lacked any cut or *chic*. 'You'll have to learn about dress. You can't meet my friends looking frowsy like that.'

Her hands slid in a little deprecating movement down the front of her dress.

'I never liked this one, but Aunt Agni said it would be very serviceable.'

'Well, you won't have to worry about dresses being

serviceable—not any more. Mother and Jenny often wear a dress only once——'

'Only once!' gasped Serra. 'I could never be as wasteful as that!'

'A ball dress is never used twice. It would be talked about for years if my wife wore a ball dress for two separate occasions.'

She blinked at him, endeavouring to assimilate this. But no matter how much consideration she gave to the matter she could not see herself buying a new ball gown if she had one in her wardrobe which had been worn on only one occasion.

'What do we do now?' Serra wanted to know. It was half past seven and she was feeling hungry. 'Do we have dinner at this time?'

'At about a quarter past eight, usually. Have you anything better than that to wear?'

'Something lighter, you mean?' She had three new dresses which her father had bought her.

'That's right.' Dirk frowned in thought. 'I should have got you some clothes. It's a wonder Charles didn't think to mention the matter.'

'Are you having your dinner with me?' she ventured to ask after a long moment of silence.

'This evening, yes. But I rarely dine at home more than once or twice a week.'

She said nothing, wondering what she would do, all by herself. However, she had no intention of dwelling on that at present, not only because she was hungry, but also because the idea of dining alone with her husband was most attractive. She had been alone with him only once since her marriage—that being during the drive from the airport after saying goodbye to Charles. Serra did not count the time when he had brought her home from the night club, for that was an incident she fervently wanted to forget.

For dinner she wore a printed summer dress, a flowered cotton thing upon which her husband instantly frowned. Preston maintained a wooden expression, but Serra cowered inwardly. Preston was more formidable than Dirk had ever been.

The table was laid with Georgian silver and Sèvres china, with ornate candelabra down the centre. The table was too large, the room too high and the austere ancestors too overpowering.

'Do you never eat in the cosy room?' she asked, waiting until Preston was out of earshot.

'The cosy room?'

'You know—the one I like best.'

'No; this is the dining-room. You can't eat in a room like that.'

She had eaten just wherever she felt like eating, Serra recalled, and mostly that was on the patio, with her kebabs and brown unsalted bread set out on a small wickerwork table under the shade of the trellised vines.

Dirk spoke little during the meal and, consequently, it did not come up to Serra's expectations. With the meal over Serra half expected Dirk to sit with her in the cosy room, but he seemed restless and said he was going out for the rest of the evening.

'What shall I do?' she asked, her spirits dampening somewhat.

'Go to bed; you must be tired after all the travelling, and the excitement of meeting your new relations.'

She had no alternative than to do as he told her; in the next room she heard him moving about for a little while and then the outer door closed. She heard his firm light footsteps on the stairs, then the voice of

Preston.

Serra heard her husband again later. He woke her up with the closing of his bedroom door. Reaching out, she switched on the gilded bedside lamp and looked at the clock. Ten minutes to five....

CHAPTER FIVE

THERE was a lag to Serra's footsteps and a droop to her mouth as she wandered down the drive and passed through the high wrought-iron gates at either side of which stood a turreted stone lodge. The dream had been so exciting, but the awakening left Serra dejected and lacking hope for a pleasant and contented future. It was better than being married to Phivos, she kept telling herself—but it certainly was not as eventful and thrilling a life as she had anticipated. Perhaps, she thought as she took the winding lane leading to the river, it would have been all right had Jenny shown some interest in her. But Jenny was fully occupied with having a good time, and with her various boy-friends.

'If I could find a boy-friend,' murmured Serra, 'life might become a little more interesting.'

And of course, if Dirk stayed in more than he did.... Life then would certainly be more interesting. But Serra did not dwell on this last idea; she must not think too much of her husband at all, because when she did her heart seemed to become filled with lead.

The river Stour wound about in the meadows; above, the sky was blue-grey but the sun was striving to break through and in a short while its autumn warmth would fill the valley. She turned to look back at the great house on the hill. Gables and columns, ivy-clad walls and warm weathered Portland stone. Lawns and fountains and statuary; terraces and formal rose gardens and wooded enclosures. How different from her father's austere villa in Greece, with its whitened walls and blue-shuttered windows. She swallowed, remembering Dirk's promise that she could go home for a visit—but he had said his sister would accompany her, and when Serra had asked Jenny about this the older girl had frowned and shrugged and said,

'Some time—but not this year.'

Delightful thatched cottages stood back from the river—the homes of estate workers. Children played in the gardens, women pegged out washing, snow-white or brightly coloured. It hung, limp, for there was no breeze as yet. Someone smiled, lifted a hand and called,

'Good morning, Mrs Morgan. It be a little colder, gettin'.'

Serra glanced towards the garden from which the sound had come. An ancient man was standing in his garden, peering at her over the hedge. 'Youse'll not be used to this 'ere weather what we've bin 'avin' just now—not with youse bein' in the sun all youse life.'

She smiled and shook her head and murmured an agreement, then continued to walk on, along the banks of the river. Was life to be like this all the while? Strange how the glamour had faded, and in so short a time. Less than two months she had been here, at the Grange... and she had never been so bored in her life. If only she could make friends. The prospect had all been so clear, on that day when, having met Dirk, she had proceeded with dogged persistence to urge him to marriage. She had visualized gathering round her many friends of her own age, of going out to parties and theatres—in fact, partaking in every pursuit that spelled freedom.

But she had done nothing except sit in the cosy room, her legs curled under her, reading, or, like this, walking in the lovely countryside of Dorset, alone. True, Mrs Morgan came over at times, but she had her own social round, her own establishment to run, and it was not to be expected that she could spare much time for her new daughter-in-law. She was kind, but too busy to entertain Serra; she advised about clothes, but could not spare the time to accompany Serra on a shopping expedition. Consequently Serra had not bought much at all, and as for spending the money Dirk allowed her—well, that was all practically intact.

She spread the mackintosh she had brought with her and sat down on the river bank. What was to be done? There must be something.... Her eyes flickered, then stared unseeingly at some twigs floating slowly along the clear water. Her mother had never mentioned relations, but.... Goodwin was her mother's maiden name, and she had lived in the Midlands. Was that a big area? Serra knit her brows in thought, recalling the name Walsall....

Perhaps she would not have troubled about finding out if she did have relations had not Dirk decided that morning to go to London.

'You said you'd be at home for a couple of days—I mean, you said you weren't even going out, because you had work to do appertaining to the estate.' To her dismay she was almost in tears; her lashes were already damp and she brushed a swift hand across them. 'It's lonely without anyone.'

Dirk frowned at her from his great height. He seemed to grow more handsome every day, she thought, staring into his eyes. If only he would take her out sometimes ... she wanted to be seen with him, so that she could feel proud. This much she knew. As yet, nothing else registered.

'I have more urgent business in London.' He continued to frown and she wondered if he were a little anxious about her. 'Hasn't Jenny been round this week?'

'This week? Jenny hasn't been here for over a fortnight.'

'She hasn't?' His mouth compressed. 'I'll go over and have a word with her. She's no right to leave you alone like this.'

She hesitated.

'Dirk ... if you would take me with you sometimes...?' Her soft sweet voice trailed away into a hopeless silence as her husband shook his head.

'You knew from the start that I'd no intention of taking you about. You must try to make your own amusement——'

'I do—reading in the cosy room all day.'

Her swift delivery and her tone of voice brought a dark lift to his brow.

'Are you complaining of your life?' he inquired, amazed. 'You have just about everything a girl could wish for! And you seem to have forgotten your gratitude!'

'No, I haven't, Dirk, b-but it isn't as I imagined it w-would be.'

'That's to be expected; you're in a strange country and naturally it'll take a bit of getting used to.'

She smiled through the mist that had covered her eyes.

'You don't understand my meaning, Dirk.'

'Then perhaps you'll explain?' But although he stood there, in a state of apparent patience, his flickering glance towards the grandfather clock in the corner was more than sufficient to reveal his true feelings and Serra merely said,

'It doesn't matter, Dirk.' And then, 'How long will

you be in London?'

'A week, maybe—or perhaps a fortnight.'

A fortnight! It was a lifetime. She said impulsively,

'Can I come with you? You can leave me,' she added breathlessly as he switched her a darkling look. 'I'll amuse myself, and I'll stay in my room in the evenings, I promise. I'll be very, very good, and no trouble to you at all. *Please* take me, Dirk!'

'It's impossible,' he almost snapped, and without affording her time to renew her pleading he turned on his heel and left the room.

And so she decided to insert her advertisement, struggling for hours in an endeavour to find the best way of wording it. And she wasn't all that satisfied with her final result, but she thought it would have the desired effect.

'Young lady, newly come from Greece, would like to contact some of her mother's relatives. Will anyone with the surname Goodwin, and living in or near Walsall, please communicate with Mrs Dirk Morgan, Chalcombe Grange, Portford Magna, Dorset?'

The advertisement was sent to a newspaper circulating in that particular area and three days later Serra was called to the telephone. This was a contingency with which she had not reckoned and by the end of the day she was exhausted, having spent practically every minute of it with the receiver in her hand. Preston was obviously curious—and disapproving, she felt sure. As for Serra herself, she was thoroughly tired by the time she went upstairs to bed, but even then there was no peace, for the calls came in until half past ten. What a good thing Dirk was away, she thought, hoping this would not happen again tomorrow. But it did. Meanwhile, at ten o'clock in the morning Preston entered the cosy room carrying a huge silver tray piled high with letters of all shapes and sizes.

'Your mail, madam,' he said, glancing oddly at her, adding, with barely smothered sarcasm, 'Perhaps I'd better leave the tray.'

'Thank you, Preston,' she returned in a small voice. She wished she weren't so apprehensive of the man. But he looked so forbidding and so grand. Serra always felt his portrait should be in the Long Gallery among the notables associated with the Grange throughout the ages. It should be in a prominent position, and enhanced by a solid gold frame with scrolls and filigree and decorated with precious stones. 'Yes, you c-can leave the tray.'

With the door closed behind him, however, her excitement knew no bounds. Were all these her relatives? In Greece so large a number of relatives was quite normal, but Serra had always been under the impression that in England families were much smaller. How very strange that her mother had never mentioned all these....

One after another she opened the letters. Some contained snapshots of handsome young men; some were from educated people, some from near-illiterates. Some were from old people who mentioned long-dead incidents of which Serra could not possibly be aware. By the time the last of the hundred or so letters was opened Serra was in a state of utter confusion. That all these were not her relatives was now seeping into her brain. What did not seep into her brain was the fact that among this pile of letters there were many from cranks, from would-be beggars—and from sharks. It did not dawn on her that the advertisement might have been much better for the insertion of a box number in preference to the very impressive address of the Grange.

After taking her lunch alone in the dining-room Serra began a sorting out, but she was not very experienced at detecting the fraudulence that clearly ran through the majority of the letters, and those she eventually picked out appeared to her innocent judgment to be the ones she must answer, and this she did, at once. Meanwhile, the telephone continued to ring, and the following day another huge batch of letters arrived. Feeling rather sick at the sight of the tray brought in by the wooden-faced butler, Serra began to wonder where this would end.

'Thank you.' She tried to sound dignified, simply as an act of defence against His Majesty, as she had come to think of him. 'Just put the tray down on the table.' The phone rang and she lifted the receiver. 'I'm rather busy,' she added, nodding a dismissal.

Preston's eyes moved almost imperceptibly from her flushed face to the tray he had put down on the table as requested.

'I'm sure you are, madam,' he agreed suavely, and with his customary gliding silence, he was gone from the room.

When on the fourth day another batch of letters arrived Serra put the whole lot into a shopping bag which she had brought with her from Greece, and, going out, dumped them into a waste bin on the side of the road where, in a lay-by, several cars had pulled up while their owners and passengers got out to stretch their legs.

'That's that!' Serra gave a deep sigh of relief. 'There *can't* be any more Goodwins living around there!'

But for several days letters poured in, though in gradually diminishing numbers. They all went into the waste bin, and it was only when the replies to her own letters came that she was really interested.

One, from a young man who had said very little in his first letter, interested her greatly and she decided to ask him to the Grange. She answered some of the others, but was cagey. Roderick Melsham, if he proved to be the cousin of her mother's niece twice removed, would help her to find any other relatives who might be around.

He arrived promptly the following afternoon after receiving her letter only a few hours earlier. He had telephoned, telling Serra when to expect him, and it was with a wildly fluttering heart that she heard Preston announce him.

'Show him into the drawing-room,' she ordered, avoiding his gaze. 'I'll be there in a few minutes.'

What was Preston thinking about all this? Did all the servants know about her huge mail—and the telephone calls? They must do; one would not have secrets in an establishment like this. Well, she thought, tossing her head as she went out into the hall, it was no concern of theirs what she did, so they could just mind their own business!

The young man was dressed soberly enough, but somehow Serra gained the impression that he was decidedly uncomfortable. His chin was red and she frowned in puzzlement until it dawned on her that he had only recently shaved off a beard. His voice, however, was quiet and cultured, his smile one of charm and pleasure. He held out a hand and Serra took it.

'Please sit down,' she invited awkwardly, indicating a chair. 'Are you really related to me?'

'I feel pretty sure of it.' His eyes wandered round the room, taking in every expensive detail before returning to Serra and resting on the third finger of her left hand for a second or two. He asked Serra questions about her mother, which she answered, and only then did he begin telling her about himself. Details linked up flawlessly with what Serra had so eagerly told him and before very long she was fully convinced her advertisement had not been wasted. She found her companion charming, and although for some incomprehensible reason she felt a little access of misgiving she shook it off, assuring herself that its cause was merely the result of the strangeness of the situation.

Roderick asked about her husband. She talked a little about Dirk, saying she was sure he'd be delighted to meet Roderick. At which Roderick frowned, much to Serra's puzzlement, and asked why Serra had been so anxious to discover her relations.

She was at a loss, because she had not given a thought to the fact that she must account for having done this all on her own. It struck her suddenly that perhaps it was not quite the thing for the squire's wife to advertise in the newspaper for relatives. If she had consulted Dirk he might have known of a better way of tackling the problem—through his lawyer, perhaps. However, there was nothing to be gained by dwelling on that now and she tried lightly to pass off the question by saying it was only natural that she should want to find some of her mother's people.

'My husband is away from home quite a lot,' she went on to explain. 'He has business matters which take up a great deal of his time and—and I thought that if I could find some relatives of my own I'd have someone to visit, and to visit me.' She smiled at him and his lids came down, hiding his expression. 'I wondered if you'd take me around? I want to visit theatres and go to dances and—things,' she ended vaguely.

'Your husband won't mind?'

'Not at all,' she blithely assured him. 'We both—I mean, he doesn't mind my having some freedom.'

Roderick leant forward and helped himself to a cigarette from the gold box, then picked up a matching lighter and flicked it to the cigarette. He held it in his hand, examining it for a moment before his eyes moved to Serra, sitting there, small and dainty, her hands clasped in her lap. Roderick's eyes narrowed as smoke went into them; he blew it away and watched it curl towards the great chimney, sucked in by the draught. Slowly he replaced the gold lighter on the table.

'I'll be only too willing to take you about.' Roderick paused a moment before pointing out that Dorset was some distance from where he lived, but Serra obligingly told him he could come and stay at the Grange. In Greece relations were always staying at the house.

'I expect you have week-ends free,' she said. 'What sort of work do you do?'

A small silence and then,

'I'm an executive,' he replied, pulling on his cigarette.

Her eyes opened appreciatively.

'That sounds very important.'

'It is, rather.'

'What kind of house do you live in?' He had already told her he was an orphan, which disappointed her, rather, because she would have liked to think she had other relatives. Roderick had a brother, but he was living in Canada, having married a Canadian girl who had come over to England last year for a holiday.

'It isn't like this,' he promptly answered, and she laughed.

'Not many people live in houses like this, I think.'

'You were lucky to marry a man of this standing. How did you come to meet him?'

Serra shrugged.

'We just met,' she said, and changed the subject, asking again if he had his week-ends free.

'Yes. I have Saturdays and Sundays free.'

'Will you come and stay here, then?'

He regarded her through half-closed eyes, a thoughtful frown on his brow.

'Is your husband away at present?' he wanted to know, ignoring her question for the moment.

'Yes—but he should be back about Monday or Tuesday.'

'Not till then? Well, I can come tomorrow evening and stay until Sunday night.'

She smiled happily.

'That'll be lovely! It's very good of you. You're sure you haven't made any other arrangements?'

'It wouldn't matter if I had,' he responded gallantly. 'I've never found a new relative before, so I must make an occasion of it.'

'Will you stay to dinner tonight?' she ventured, but he shook his head, saying he had a long journey in front of him, and after they had taken afternoon tea together he said goodbye, promising to return the following evening.

Serra did a little dance round her room as she dressed for dinner an hour or two later. A real relation! She could do without Jenny now. Roderick would know what to do about meeting people; very soon her dream would be realized and she would have made some nice friends of her own.

Preston's face was a study when, the following afternoon, Serra told him to see that a room was prepared for a friend of hers, and that the friend was a male.

'He'll be here in time for dinner,' she said, hoping she sounded haughty as she added, 'Dinner might have to be later than usual—please bear that in mind, Preston.' So much for His Majesty! He now knew she could give him an order.

Over dinner Serra told Roderick about the stacks of letters she had received in reply to her advertisement. His eyes flickered but, strangely, he did not appear half so surprised as she would have expected.

'How did you pick mine out?' he wanted to know, eyeing the silver plate in an oddly thoughtful way.

'I honestly don't know. I chose several at first, and answered them. Then when you replied I liked the sound of your letter.' She gave him a delectable smile. 'I had realized by this time that some of the letters weren't genuine, but yours did sound genuine—and it was!'

Roderick beckoned for more wine, his expression hidden from Serra as he watched the sparkling liquid rise in his glass.

After dinner they walked in the grounds, making plans for the following day. Roderick had come by train, having a taxi from the station, but Serra said they could go out in one of the cars, which were in the garage. It would be quite all right to take one, she decided, for hadn't Dirk said she could do as she liked?

On returning to the house Roderick helped himself to a drink and sat down with it, his eyes hidden from Serra as he said,

'You haven't shown me over this lovely home of yours.'

She smiled and said they would go on a tour the following morning.

'There are wonderful things here,' she added enthusiastically. 'You'll be thrilled with all the treasures.'

'I'm sure I shall.' He took the gold lighter from the table and held it to his cigarette. And once again he kept it in his hand, looking at it for a long while before returning it to the table. 'In fact, I'd love to have a look round now.'

'There's such a lot,' she began doubtfully. 'It will take ages.'

'In that case,' he smiled, 'we had better do it now— if we're going out for the whole day tomorrow. We shall want to be off early.' They had decided to go to Bournemouth for the day, and had already said they would set off immediately after breakfast.

'All right,' agreed Serra, getting up. 'I'll show you round now.'

As they came into the hall Preston emerged from somewhere and silently disappeared into another room.

'Does that fellow always prowl around like that?' Roderick asked sharply.

'He isn't prowling.' Odd that she should resent her cousin's phrasing, especially as she so disliked the butler. 'He's doing his job, I suppose,' she added vaguely.

Serra took Roderick into the magnificent dining-room, where he seemed particularly interested in the fine Meissen china and beautiful silver candelabra. He examined the pictures and ornaments, and an eighteenth-century gilt salver. The next room was the breakfast room, then the Chinese Room, but it was in the Silver Room that he appeared to be most interested, giving a little gasp on entering, a gasp which he instantly tried to cover by a sudden cough.

There were masses of Georgian silver in the form of candlesticks and trays and condiment sets. There were several solid gold teapots with matching cream jugs and sugar basins; there were exquisite bread-baskets and dressing-sets. All were set out on shelves or on priceless silver-inlaid tables.

'Aren't they beautiful?' Serra watched his face, smiling at his expression. 'They took my breath away at first.'

'They take mine away,' he admitted, then frowned suddenly. 'Did you hear anything?' He seemed nervous all at once, she thought, seeing him turn swiftly to look at the open door.

'No, I didn't hear anything.'

'That butler—I'm sure he's still around. Hasn't he got his own place? I mean, surely he doesn't just walk about the house all the time?'

'He isn't about.' Serra became faintly uneasy, although she could not have said why. 'I don't know what you mean?'

'I'm sure he was at that door. The fellow wants putting in his place; he's only a servant.'

Serra glanced away, once again resenting her cousin's remarks about the butler.

'Shall we go back to the drawing-room?' she said, deciding she did not want to show Roderick any more of the house. He agreed and they sat talking and drinking—at least Roderick was drinking. And far too much, she thought, wondering if her husband would want his whisky to be taken like this.

'Is there any chance of your husband coming home earlier than he said?' Roderick's soft voice broke into Serra's thoughts and she looked swiftly at him.

'No, I shouldn't think so.'

'He could come tomorrow.' The words were scarcely audible; Serra had the impression that Roderick had spoken his thoughts aloud.

'He said Monday or Tuesday, so I don't expect he will change his plans.'

Roderick was thoughtful; Serra began to talk about tomorrow's projected outing, but he now appeared to have lost interest and merely answered her in monosyllables. However he did ask about the car they would use and she said there was a Rover and a Jaguar. Her husband had taken the Mercedes, she told him.

'A Jag, eh? It's in the garage, you say?'

'Yes—that's the building I pointed out, if you remember?'

'But the door will be kept locked?'

She frowned in puzzlement.

'It might be, but it doesn't matter. Preston will give me the key in the morning.'

For some reason she could not fathom Roderick was shaking his head.

'I've just remembered I've a phone call to make,' he said. 'Is there a box anywhere close?'

She blinked at him.

'You can phone from here.'

'I feel like a breath of fresh air, so I might as well walk to a box. Is there one?' he asked again.

'Yes, at the end of the lane....' She noticed her hand trembling; her arm was resting along the arm of the chair and she assumed she was pressing on a nerve. She moved her arm, but her hand still trembled. So did the nerves of her stomach. She was alert, and frightened, although her fears were vague and inexplicable.

'I'll go, then.' He stood up, smiling at her. His face was open and frank, she thought, and yet....

'I m-might be in bed when you get back.'

'That's all right. I know where my room is. Good night, Serra, sleep tight!'

'Good night.' Something made her say, 'Tomorrow —we are going out for the day?'

'Of course. I'm very much looking forward to it.' But Roderick avoided her eyes....

She lay in bed, but sleep would not come. And as in the darkness her fears increased unaccountably, she sat up and switched on the light. It was only eleven o'clock; Preston would not have gone to bed. Why should she have a thought like that? But Serra was seeing Roderick in the Silver Room; she saw again his expression as he took in all the treasure there. She saw his uneasiness and heard again his comments about Preston's being at the door. Neither she nor Roderick had seen Preston ... and yet Roderick had the impression that the butler was around. Had he been standing at the open door, watching them? Suddenly Serra knew that Preston did not trust her cousin and, instead of feeling indignant, as should have been her natural reaction, she experienced an odd relief. But it did not last and she reached out for the telephone. But whom could she ring? 'I'm being silly,' she said, and replaced the receiver. But why should Roderick go out to phone? And this was surely an odd time to remember he had a call to make? Serra's fear now became very strong—and it was no longer inexplicable. She knew nothing at all about Roderick....

'Oh, supposing he isn't honest. Supposing he's—he's a crook....' Serra's heart gave a jerk at the idea and naturally her thoughts went to her husband. One more scrape, he had said....

'I'm being fanciful—whom can I ring? Of course Roderick's all right——' She put a brake on her inconsistent mumblings and tried to collect her thoughts, but all the while she was seeing clues that led clearly to the fact that Roderick was not what he appeared to be. The car—he had seemed to think that Preston would not let her have the key of the garage. Prior to that Roderick had asked if her husband was likely to return the following day. It was still puzzling, but

Serra was now convinced that her 'cousin' was not straight. She slipped out of bed, but her legs were weak. Nevertheless she got dressed, but after that all she could do was walk about the bedroom, having visions of being shot or knocked out should she move through the door. She looked at the phone several times. The police? She dared not! Preston? No, not Preston. Mrs Morgan—yes, Mrs Morgan!

There was no reply for a while and then a maid answered the phone. Serra knew she had got the girl up out of bed.

'No, she isn't here, Mrs Morgan. She and Miss Jenny will be very late; they've gone to a party.'

'Thank you. I'm sorry to have disturbed you.'

'That's all right, madam. Good night.'

'Good night.' Serra looked at the receiver for a long while. Charles! Charles would know what to do. Why hadn't she thought of him before? She did not know his number, but she knew where he lived, and a few minutes after the operator had given her the number she was waiting agitatedly for someone to answer the phone. Supposing Charles were with Dirk? 'If he isn't in then I'll get Preston to ring Dirk,' she whispered, trembling all over now. Yes, loath as she was to petition help from Preston she knew she must. She could have by-passed him, but she herself had no idea where her husband was. A voice at the other end of the line ... Serra asked for Mr Kershawe.

'Who is speaking?' asked the voice, and Serra sagged with relief.

'Mrs Morgan—Serra Morgan.'

'Just one minute; I'll tell Mr Kershawe.'

For a long moment after hearing Charles's rather troubled 'Serra, what on earth is it?' Serra could not speak. And then it all tumbled out, not very coherently, because Charles kept on interrupting to ask a question.

'Come, Charles, please come at once! I'm terrified!'

'But Preston——'

'I want *you*!'

'But, Serra, I'm miles away. Preston is the man you want. Lord, girl, how did you come to get into a mess like this? Dirk will cast you off——'

'Oh,' she quivered, 'you're heartless to remind me of that just now! If you don't come I'll never speak to you again.'

'All right, but I still think you should tell Preston of your fears. He'd know exactly what to do.'

'He doesn't approve of me.'

'What's that to do with it? He's not going to let Dirk be robbed just because he doesn't like his wife.'

'Are you c-coming or—or n-not——' A little sob escaped her and Charles said a hurried, 'Okay, I'll be there—but I'll probably break my neck—certainly I'll be run in for breaking the speed limit!' and rang off.

She sat on her bed, watching the clock. Charles lived near Bath, but the roads would be very quiet and he should be here in half an hour. He arrived in twenty-five minutes. She heard his car and opened the window.

'Can you come up the fire-escape?' she called softly.

'Why all the melodrama?' he wanted to know a few seconds later on stepping through her window. 'Preston would have let me in.'

'I don't want Preston to know. You'll think of something, Charles, and even Dirk will never know.' Charles's presence had lifted the blight enormously. She had previously resigned herself to her husband's wrath, but now she cherished the hope that her foolishness could be kept from him. She looked up at

Charles. 'I'm so glad to see you!'

'Yes, Serra, no doubt you are, but this can't be dealt with quietly.' He paused. 'How do you know this Roderick's crooked?'

'I'm not sure, granted.' Serra went on to explain the whole, for her information on the telephone had been scrappy, to say the least. 'He might be all right,' she ended, 'but I have a dreadful feeling that he isn't.'

'Now you've told me everything I'm damned sure he isn't!' Charles's face was grim and censorious. 'What made you do it—advertise, I mean? Why didn't you discuss the matter with Dirk first?'

She gave him a wry glance.

'Dirk never has time to bother with me,' she said on a tiny note of self-pity.

'Well, he'll certainly have time to bother with you over this! It can't be kept from him, Serra.'

'It can! I'm relying on you. Frighten Roderick away —or—or something.'

'Where is he now?'

'I expect he's in his room, waiting until everyone's in bed. Do you think he phoned an accomplice?'

'Nothing so sure.' Charles became thoughtful. 'It's all very clear now,' he announced at last. 'He was all set to do the job at his leisure, probably tomorrow night when you returned from your trip. He'd have the car, he was thinking—which he would ditch later. But he suddenly realized that Preston suspected him and began to wonder if he'd ring Dirk, or perhaps the police. So he decided it must be a rush job——'

'You feel sure that Preston suspected him, then?'

'I'm sure Preston was following you around the house and this fellow knew it. That's why he was nervous when you were in the Silver Room—Preston was there, you can be sure of it, but he buzzed out of the way sharpish before either of you saw him. Later when you were talking Roderick knew instinctively that Preston would never give you the key to the garage, and that was the moment he decided to do the job in a hurry. Hence his phoning for an accomplice to bring some sort of vehicle.' Charles shook his head and his expression was as formidable as any Serra had seen on her husband's face as he added, 'You must have been out of your mind to allow a stranger like this to go all over the house, taking stock of everything.'

'I know that now,' she agreed forlornly. 'You see, in Greece we trust everybody.'

'Well, I don't know why you should. I expect they have as much crime as anyone else.'

'I haven't come up against it.'

Charles sighed exasperatedly.

'No use feeling sorry for yourself, Serra. You should think before you act. It seems to me that impulsiveness is your greatest failing.'

She nodded.

'I fear it is,' and she added in a small voice, 'It's no excuse that I was lonely.'

Charles softened, and patted her shoulder. It was a kindly act, but thoughtless, for it was bound to release Serra's pent-up emotions, and before he knew what was happening she was weeping against his chest. His arms went round her protectingly and soothingly, and he murmured,

'There, there, don't cry. No real damage has been done——' Breaking off as the door swung wide open, he looked over Serra's head to meet her husband's smouldering and incredulous gaze.

'What the——?' Dirk strode into the room and as Serra twisted round, her eyes widened with fright, he took her by the shoulders and wrenched her away from the protecting arms of his friend. 'Perhaps,' he said furiously, 'one of you will tell me what this is all about!'

'Dirk! How did you get here—oh, you're hurting me!'

'Hurting you! I'll break your damned neck! What's going on, I said!'

'Steady on, Dirk,' intervened Charles in his customary mild tones. 'First of all, tell us why you're here?' The merest pause of enlightenment and then, 'Preston rang you?'

Dirk's nostrils flared.

'What,' he blazed, 'are you doing in my wife's bedroom?'

A profound silence fell before Charles said curiously,

'The pose of outraged husband seems totally unsuited to the situation, Dirk. You married for convenience, remember?' And when for one wrathful second Dirk seemed incapable of speech, 'Greek girls don't,' came Charles's gentle reminder. 'You said so yourself; or have you forgotten?'

'Answer my question. What are you doing here!'

'I sent for him,' confessed Serra, lifting a tear-stained face to her husband's dark countenance. 'He came up the fire-escape.'

'How very original! What about your other boyfriend?' She merely looked indignantly at him and he said, 'Why did you send for Charles?'

'She'd begun to suspect this fellow—her cousin——'

'Her—*what*?'

'I'd better explain,' began Serra, but of course she was not allowed to do so.

'Where did you pick this rogue up?'

'Perhaps you'll let *me* explain,' interposed Charles

mildly, moving across the room to close the door. 'But first of all, I am right in assuming that Preston phoned you?'

'He phoned me a couple of hours ago. I've been booked twice for speeding!'

Serra looked fearfully at him—and moved closer to Charles, who said commiseratingly,

'Hard luck. I managed to get away with it.' And he couldn't help adding, 'You wretch, Serra! If Dirk beats you it'll be no more than you deserve. You promised to be so good, and not let Dirk even feel he was married.'

Serra's lip quivered. She wanted to ask Dirk if he intended sending her home, but the blockage in her throat prevented speech. In any case, Charles was speaking and soon Dirk had heard all that happened. He looked quite ready to explode when at length his friend lapsed into silence.

'You advertised——and actually gave my address! Have you no sense at all?'

Serra started to cry.

'I was lonely,' she protested. 'How did I know you had such rogues in your country? I wish I was back in Greece where p-people are honest!'

Dirk smothered a curse.

'You don't wish it any more than I do!'

'You should have married Clarice!'

'You're quite right, I should.' But this time Dirk's tone lacked the vehemence he had shown up till now and Charles intervened, saying,

'Shall we get down to something constructive? We're all agreed about this Roderick being a rogue, but we haven't any real proof, so what are we to do about him?'

'Preston was mean and interfering to send for you,'

Serra interrupted, looking at her husband, and received a scowling glance for her trouble.

'You should be grateful to Preston,' Dirk declared. 'He must have been puzzled by all these letters Charles says you received, and when this Roderick appeared he probably concluded his presence had something to do with the letters. He was very vague—and guarded, let me tell you,' he added forcefully as if to acquaint Serra with the fact that Preston was not the interfering person she had declared him to be. 'He merely said he didn't like this man and asked me if he should keep an eye on him.'

'I still think he should have minded his own business!'

'No doubt you do. It's pretty obvious from the fact of your sending for Charles that you hoped to keep this escapade from me.'

'Are—are y-you going to s-send me home?' she just could not help asking, and received a short and sharp 'yes' in undelayed response. Her tears flowed again and another smothered curse issued from her husband's lips.

'While you two are throwing bricks at one another the man could be running off with all the family heirlooms,' began Charles.

'I'm not throwing bricks,' protested Serra, casting Charles an indignant glance. But her thoughts were elsewhere. To be sent home in disgrace. What would her father say? Such a thing was unheard of in Greece. And Aunt Agni—how she would gloat, because even with the wedding date fixed she had asserted that the marriage would never take place. They were complete opposites, she had said. They would never get on together.

'Serra,' came Dirk's voice, soft now and yet vibrantly

dangerous, 'if you interrupt once more I'll box your ears.' He turned to Charles. 'The fellow won't be running off with the family heirlooms at all, because he's gone.'

'Gone?' echoed his two listeners simultaneously.

'Took fright because when he returned from his walk Preston remained hovering around, even following when he went upstairs to the room you'd given him—the best guest room, he added, although there was no need to, Serra thought. 'A little later he opened the door, only to find Preston posted at the end of the corridor. A few minutes later he emerged with his belongings and said he'd just telephoned a friend at home and he had to leave. Preston escorted him to the front door and secured it after him. He'll probably meet up with this accomplice you appear to think he had.' Dirk spoke to Charles, but every now and then he sent his wife such darkling glances that by the time he had finished she was again incapable of speech, even had she been able to find anything to say. Nevertheless, she was inordinately relieved at this turn of events because she'd had visions of the police being called in and the whole thing getting into the newspapers for all Dirk's friends to read.

'Well,' murmured Charles mildly at last, 'as there's no damage done how about retiring to the drawing-room and having a drink?'

Serra sent him a grateful glance, but her heart was heavy.

'I don't feel like drinking,' she said miserably. 'I haven't anything to celebrate, for I don't know what my father will say when I arrive home.'

'Nor do I,' rejoined her husband heartlessly. 'Much less do I care. Come, Charles, your suggestion's a good one—though a drink will hardly compensate for what

I've missed.'

'You mean,' faltered Serra with her incurable impulsiveness, 'that you left your girl-friend?'

Her husband glared at her, hesitated a second and then,

'Yes,' he said between his teeth, 'I left my girl-friend!'

CHAPTER SIX

Serra had made her escape from the oppressive silence of the breakfast-room over an hour ago and she was still wandering about the grounds, expecting all the time to hear her husband's summons and his orders for her to go upstairs and pack her belongings.

Perhaps he was phoning the airport, she thought, to find out if there was a plane that day.

A movement in the distant grove brought her attention to the girl on the horse, cantering through the trees, making for the Grange. Serra would have sought refuge in a nearby summerhouse, but Jenny had seen her and she stopped walking and waited for her sister-in-law to come up to her.

'Good morning,' greeted Jenny, smiling.

Serra returned the greeting, but abstractedly, for her mind was on other things. And because she was not in clear control of her thoughts she added,

'You're out early—seeing that you were so late in last night.'

'How do you know?' demanded Jenny in surprise.

'I rang your maid,' Serra was forced to admit.

'You wanted me?'

'No—your mother. It was nothing,' she said quickly, wishing Jenny would not look down at her like that, seeming to be so arrogant and distantly superior. 'He has a lovely silky coat.' Serra managed a difficult smile, but it was owing to the activities of the horse, for it was nuzzling her shoulder.

'*He* happens to be a she.'

'Oh....' Serra had no wish to stand here talking to

Jenny, who, she thought, should have dismounted, not continued to sit up there, looking haughty. 'I'll be going now. I'm—I'm just taking a walk.'

'What's wrong?' Jenny sprang down and stood, one hand carelessly thrown across the horse's back, the other holding the reins, which she thoughtfully looped and twisted in her fingers. 'You've been crying.'

'Not recently.' The rather abstracted rejoinder told Jenny nothing and to Serra's surprise the older girl asked for an explanation. 'It was last night—and in the night,' Serra answered, her voice caught on a little sob.

'Dirk?'

Serra blinked.

'What do you mean?'

'What's Dirk been doing to you?' And, when Serra just shook her head, 'He must have done something to make you cry.'

Why should Jenny trouble to question her? wondered Serra. After showing scarcely any interest at all she was now eager to know what had been happening to make Serra cry. Short of snubbing Jenny, which she had no desire to do, Serra could only offer a full, if brief, explanation of what had occurred, feeling that Jenny would find out in any case because if she was so close to her brother he would obviously take his troubles to her.

To Serra's surprise Jenny's face was dark with anger when she had finished speaking. She snapped,

'Dirk was in London, was he? What doing?'

'I don't know——'

'And you didn't even know where he was, I suppose?'

'No, but that wasn't important. Dirk is under no obligation to tell me where he is.'

'No?' Jenny's eyes glinted. 'Supposing you were to be ill, or were to have an accident?'

Serra frowned.

'What has that to do with it?'

'Plenty! A wife should at least know where to find her husband!' There was a strange and awful emphasis on the 'at least' which seemed to say that in Jenny's opinion Dirk should not be away at all, but at home with his wife.

'You know the reason for our marriage,' Serra reminded her and added, as though compelled by some force, 'Your mother said you would take me under your wing, and show me around.' With the words spoken Serra realized her lack of tact and hid her face in the horse's neck, still caressing his coat. She would have liked to learn to ride, but when she had mentioned this to Dirk he had merely said she could do—some time.

'Are you saying that had I taken you under my wing, as you put it, this would not have happened?'

'No—certainly not! I'm sorry if I spoke without thinking....' She tailed off, shrugging helplessly.

'So you do blame me?'

'Not blame.' She looked at her sister-in-law through misty eyes. 'I was so lonely,' she whispered. 'There wasn't anything to do——' Automatically she twisted round and looked up at the magnificent pile that was her husband's ancestral home. 'It's all so strange—and big, and—and I d-don't know anybody.' Jenny's glance was keen and swift before she also looked towards the house, and her mouth was now compressed, but Serra scarcely noticed as she went on to mention something she had deliberately left out of her previous narrative, 'It doesn't matter any more, though, because I'm going home.'

Jenny's head jerked.

'What did you say?'

'I'm g-going home——' Serra broke off as the tears fell from her eyes. 'Dirk's h-had enough of m-me.'

An astounded silence followed; the reins came down almost viciously on Jenny's protected leg.

'Home! Sending you home!' Jenny actually gritted her teeth and Serra seemed to notice her manner for the first time. She was furious. Had she a champion? wondered Serra, her heart leaping. Jenny was the last one from whom she would have expected help.

'Is Dirk in now?' rasped Jenny, fastening the reins to a gate leading off into a tree-lined walk.

'Yes, but——'

'Then by all means let us go and have a talk to him!'

Serra was soon trotting to catch up with her sister-in-law, whose own pace could only be described as a march. She was so slender and almost frail-looking, thought Serra, glancing up at her. Her hair was long and straight and held in the nape of her neck by a small black velvet bow; her features were firm but small, her skin fair and clear and transparent.

'Jenny,' began Serra a little fearfully as they neared the house, 'Dirk will be angry with me for telling you all about it. Perhaps you'd better not talk to him after all.' She was reluctant to say this, for she did feel that Jenny could influence her brother.

'No doubt about his anger,' responded Jenny in a grim voice. 'Nevertheless, I do intend talking to him. Come on, you've nothing to fear while I'm here.'

Dirk was upstairs; Jenny called and he came to the balustrade and looked down.

'What the devil do you want at this time of the morning?' he demanded. 'Go home; I've enough on my plate!'

'On your plate?' mildly. 'I want to talk to you, Dirk—and at once!'

Serra, standing at the bottom of the wide staircase beside Jenny, could only stare unbelievingly as Dirk, with a little muttered oath, came down to his sister.

'So Serra's been talking to you, has she?' Dirk glared at his wife before swinging on his heel and leading the way into the small apartment which Serra had named the cosy room. 'If you'd done as I asked,' he went on the moment they were inside and the door had closed behind Serra, 'this would never have happened.'

Jenny tossed her hat on to the couch and looked up at him.

'Why should I concern myself with her? She's your responsibility.'

Blushing at this plain speaking, and at the way Jenny referred to Serra as her and she, Serra averted her head, feeling inferior and wishing she could leave these two to argue it out on their own.

'Responsibility?' Dirk's voice was clipped and curt. 'There was to be no question of responsibility. Serra wanted her freedom; she wanted to come to England and I brought her. As far as I'm concerned the matter ends there.'

A swift intake of her breath from Jenny. Serra broke in, trying to be helpful.

'What Dirk says is quite right, Jenny. He doesn't owe me any attention because it's not really a marriage. It's just as if he brought me to England and—well, and left me.'

Jenny stared at her.

'Rubbish,' she snapped. 'Dirk is a husband, and he must accept the responsibilities of a husband.'

Dirk's eyes glinted dangerously, but his sister was not in the least disturbed by this. Meanwhile, Serra was looking from one to the other as an idea gradually began to form in her mind. Jenny had left her to her own devices, despite the fact of both her mother and brother asking her to help Serra fit into her new environment. Dirk had once said that he did not know why Jenny and he were close because Jenny disapproved of his way of life. Could it be that Jenny had acted in a way designed to change Dirk's way of life? Could it be that Jenny had deliberately kept away so that her brother would have no option than to shoulder the responsibility of a wife? If this were so it fully explained Jenny's refusal to help her sister-in-law; it also revealed her to be a much more attractive person than that of the indifferent and rather haughty girl Serra had branded her. A sudden warmth encompassed Serra and she smiled at Jenny, but Jenny was looking at Dirk, her censorious gaze unflinchingly meeting the gleam of anger in his eyes.

'The situation does not concern you,' he was saying abruptly. 'As Serra says, I don't owe her any attention —she knew this and accepted it,' he added as Jenny would have interrupted. 'So you will oblige me by keeping out of it.' Dirk glanced at his wife. 'Did you have to chatter to Jenny? I should have thought you'd want the matter to be kept quiet.'

Serra hung her head. Jenny looked at her for a long moment before returning her attention to her brother.

'Have you no heart, Dirk? Serra's a stranger in this country. She's been left on her own for over two months——'

'I asked you to take her around,' he interrupted shortly. 'It's a woman she needs, not me.'

'Would you like to have your husband's company, Serra?' came the unexpected inquiry from Jenny, and Serra's head came up. She gave a little trembling sigh as she met Dirk's gaze.

'I would, yes,' she quivered, but added, 'I know I can't have it, though, because of our bargain.'

Dirk was standing by the window, facing the two girls. He was still angry, but Serra gained the impression that he would never dream of quarrelling with Jenny. His gaze moved as Serra spoke and he frowned. But there was an almost imperceptible softening of his face and a trembling smile touched Serra's lips. Dirk sighed and shook his head.

'Have you told Jenny everything?' he asked at length. 'Have you told her I threatened to send you home?'

'Yes——'

'Home,' cut in Jenny shortly. 'This is Serra's home.'

'All right, Jenny, for heaven's sake let's forget the matter. I had no intention of sending her back to Greece anyway—naturally I hadn't.'

Both Serra and Jenny looked swiftly at him.

'Dirk, how could you frighten me like that?' Serra's voice broke even though her heart leapt at his words. 'I've been almost out of my mind wondering what Father would say.'

He seemed staggered by her admission, and now his face did soften, considerably.

'You surely didn't take me seriously?'

'Of course she did! Serra's honest herself and she takes it for granted everyone else is the same. In future don't say things you don't mean. Even I thought you meant it.'

Serra was so happy at Dirk's admission that she spoke without thinking, asking if he hadn't meant what he said about Clarice, too.

'Clarice?' Jenny looked swiftly at her brother. 'Do you know Clarice, Serra?'

'I've heard of her,' returned Serra imperturbably. 'Last night Dirk said he wished he'd married her...' She allowed her voice to trail away into the silence as Dirk's eyes glinted.

'If you'd married her,' said his sister with significant emphasis, 'you wouldn't have got away with leaving her all on her own.'

'That's the reason I didn't marry her,' responded Dirk, amused all at once.

'So you didn't mean it?' Serra lifted her face to his. Again he sighed and shook his head.

'You should have known I didn't mean it.'

She spread her hands.

'Don't you mean anything you say?' she couldn't help asking, her voice indignant and accusing because of the misery she had been through, a misery that had kept her awake throughout the night.

'I meant it when I threatened to box your ears. If I have one more experience of your stupidity then, believe me, Serra, you'll feel sorry for yourself.'

'Take no notice of him,' advised Jenny calmly, noting the sudden rush of colour that had fused Serra's cheeks. 'His bark's always been worse than his bite.' She sat down on the arm of the settee and became thoughtful for a space. 'I think you'll agree with me, Dirk,' she began reasonably, 'that Serra must be—guided a little?' And when he inclined his head in agreement, 'I'm willing to do my share ... but only if you're willing to do yours.' She smiled sweetly at him. 'We take it in turns, so to speak.'

'But—no, Jenny. The arrangement was for Dirk to go his own way. I promised that he wouldn't even know he was married.'

Not unnaturally this led to laughter; it also swept away the remnants of Dirk's ill-humour.

'I certainly know I'm married,' he retorted, speaking to Jenny but looking at his wife, who swallowed and blurted out without thinking,

'I'm sorry you had to come away from your girl-friend, but Preston needn't have rung you. Charles would have known what to do.' Her eyes strayed to Jenny, who was frowning heavily.

'So you were with a girl-friend?'

'Of course.' A challenge in his tone, and a sudden glint of danger in his eyes. His sister could go further than most people, Serra concluded, but knew that even Jenny could only go to certain lengths.

'I can't for the life of me think what you get out of all these girls,' said Jenny, still frowning at her brother.

He raised his brows, regarding her with some amusement.

'I wouldn't expect you to, Jenny,' he returned suavely.

'You take after Father!'

'So Mother says. She had a dreadful time with him.'

Jenny examined his face—then smiled to herself.

'You won't go as far as he did,' she asserted, and her brother promptly said, with a laugh,

'The wish is father to the thought, I take it?'

She looked away.

'I'm one of those foolish sisters who idolizes her brother. And as I'm an idealist also I live in continual hope that one day you'll become the brother I really want.'

The confession led to a profound silence, and the singing of birds outside was the only sound for a few moments before Dirk said, in strangely emotional tones,

'I feel, my dear, that we shall both be quite old before that day arrives.'

Jenny's eyes moved to Serra, and remained on her face for a while before examining her lovely figure, from the long arched neck to the alluring curves and the incredibly small waist.

'We shall see, Dirk,' she murmured cryptically. 'I have an idea that we won't be all that old—in fact, I have a feeling you'll mend your ways quite soon.' And, as Dirk made no comment, 'This question of Serra—are you willing to take it in turns?'

'I've no time.'

'Then neither have I.'

A faltering step took Serra closer to Jenny. She looked at her entreatingly.

'Please ... I'll be quite satisfied with your helping me. It wasn't in our bargain that Dirk would take me around.'

Avoiding her eyes, Jenny said,

'I'm sorry, but if Dirk isn't willing to give you any of his time then I'm not, either.'

Instinctively Serra knew what was in her sister-in-law's mind. She *did* want her brother to accept some responsibility, and that was because Jenny concluded it would, for part of the time at least, keep her brother out of mischief.

Dirk was glaring at his sister.

'Is that an ultimatum?' he snapped.

'Certainly it is.'

He smiled suddenly, and his expression changed.

'You'll never reform me, Jen.'

So he too knew what Jenny was about. Serra was not surprised, for Jenny had not approached the matter with any element of diplomacy.

'What is your decision?' she inquired, regarding Dirk challengingly.

A sharp intake of his breath and then,

'I must have been out of my mind to marry her! To think I concluded that she was meek and docile and wouldn't give me the least trouble!'

'Then all I can say is you didn't look very far ahead,' rejoined his sister practically. 'It should have occurred to you at once that there would be difficulties. No girl wants to spend her life alone in a rambling house like this, reading all day, or taking the odd stroll in the garden.' She turned to Serra. 'Didn't you give the matter a thought, either?'

Serra shook her head.

'I was too eager to be free, to get to England. I somehow imagined I'd have people around me, and make friends. Then I'd be invited to parties, and attend balls—and even have a nice boy-friend,' she added with her incurable honesty. Dirk frowned at this, which was strange, she thought, because he did not care in the least what she did.

'You don't have boy-friends when you're married,' said Jenny, also frowning darkly.

'You'll have discovered that Jen's a prude,' Dirk smiled, slanting a glance at his wife.

'She's right—in the ordinary way,' Serra was driven to defend her sister-in-law. 'It's just that our marriage isn't normal,' she supplemented unnecessarily.

'Well, normal or not, you're both married, and you'll have to change your way of life, Dirk. Either you forfeit some of this barren round of gaiety or else you must be prepared for trouble.' She paused a moment as if to give strength to her next words. 'Have you thought what a fool you're going to look if Serra begins having boy-friends?'

'She's not having boy-friends,' he declared with emphasis. 'She can enjoy herself in other ways.'

'She has an awful long way to go,' murmured Jenny in significant tones. 'At eighteen one wants the company of the opposite sex.'

It struck Serra that Jenny was not being very consistent, but of course she was aiming at bringing off her plan.

Dirk drew an exasperated breath.

'Charles might take her around a bit,' he suggested at last, but Jenny was shaking her head.

'No go, Dirk. You or else...'

A long silence. Serra wanted to break in and say obligingly that it did not matter but she knew that Jenny would be angry if she did, so she prudently held her tongue.

'Very well,' Dirk agreed at last, but with an audible gritting of his teeth. 'I'll give up a couple of days a week.'

'Three,' murmured Jenny, idly fingering the hat that lay on the couch. 'Three for you and four for me.' Her long lashes fluttered as she cocked him a glance, and her mouth was curved in a faint smile.

'Three!' He shook his head. 'That's half my life. Not likely!'

Jenny shrugged and, rising, picked up her hat.

'There doesn't seem any use prolonging this fruitless argument.' She smiled at Serra. 'Try not to get into too much mischief,' she said, and turned to the door.

'Jenny....' Tears started to Serra's eyes. 'Please—I don't want to trouble Dirk. Please take me around.'

Jenny's eyes were on her brother's face. She lowered her head after a moment because of the triumph in her eyes. Dirk snapped,

'Three days, then! Although I don't know why she

couldn't entertain herself for at least one day a week!'

'Of course I co——'

'That's settled then,' interrupted Jenny with a darkling glance at her sister-in-law, as she came back into the room. 'All that remains is for us to sort out the arrangements. I can't be with Serra on Tuesdays because I go to Felicity's for the day—it's a long-standing date. But as for the rest of the week——' She shrugged obligingly. 'Take your pick, Dirk.'

'Thank you!' again through gritted teeth. Serra became utterly miserable, feeling that Dirk's company, given so grudgingly, was going to be far from enjoyable. 'I want to have my week-ends free.'

And so it was arranged that Dirk should not go out on Mondays, Tuesdays and Thursdays. Jenny smiled with satisfaction as she silently dwelt on her triumph. Serra wondered how long the arrangement would last, for she felt sure Dirk would tire of her company very soon.

CHAPTER SEVEN

THEY had driven down through Bloxworth Heath, a delightful woodland region with the chalk hills rising to the north. Dirk was driving the Jaguar, with Serra sitting beside him. It had been a silent journey for the most part, but now and then Serra would speak and Dirk would reply, even though in short and rather bored accents. It was their first outing together since the 'arrangement' was made, for on Monday and Tuesday Dirk had stayed around the house, keeping Serra company, but, she surmised, bent on making her so bored she would not desire his company again. To-day, however, the sun was shining and after lunch Dirk himself had suggested a run out in the car. Quietly Serra had agreed, wishing to tell him that he need not bother unless he himself wanted to go out, but at the same time fearing that Jenny would not be pleased if Dirk should succeed in freeing himself of his part of the obligation.

'The scenery's beautiful,' she murmured as they approached the coast. 'I like the green very much.'

'We'll go to Portland Island,' he said, without much interest. 'Then we'll make for Lulworth Cove.'

Portland Island was an austere region of solid limestone where ancient marine life lay fossilized in its quarried walls. Dirk parked the car and he and Serra walked on to the raised beach that formed the back of the shore. Giant blocks of stone had been wrenched away from the main mass and these lay in wild and formidable confusion all about the shore, or piled up by the cliffs, where other giant blocks had been dislodged by the powerful waves that lashed the coast. Portland Bill jutted out into the sea, with the freakish Pulpit Rock forming a dramatic obelisk which was a reminder of early cubist carvings. A coloured lighthouse towered above, outlined sharply against the blue of a Dorset sky. The backing cliffs were rugged and massive with yawning chasms and great wide platforms.

Dirk and Serra climbed from one of the platforms to a higher vantage point from where a magnificent view could be had of several features of the coast.

'That's the Chesil Beach,' Dirk told her, indicating the great arc to their left. 'And that is Weymouth.'

'Can you swim there?' she wanted to know.

'Sure—but I don't suppose you would want to, not after the warm waters of Greece.'

'Is it very cold?'

'I think you would find it so.'

'I'd like to try—not today, of course, but some time.'

'We will, then,' he promised, and she gave him a swift smile.

'Dirk....'

'Yes?'

'You are happy? I mean, I should feel awful if I thought you were miserable, taking me out like this.'

They were high above the swelling sea, just the two of them, standing against the massive cliffs. He looked down at her and smiled.

'I'm not miserable, Serra, far from it—strangely.' He caught his lip on uttering the last word and Serra had the impression that he regretted the inclusion of it.

'I think I'm a great trouble to you, all the same,' she said, bringing her gaze from the sea to glance up at him.

He laughed and unexpectedly ruffled her hair.

'Self-pity? Or is it remorse?'

She thought for a moment.

'A little of both,' she owned, responding to his laugh.

From Portland Island they drove to Lulworth Cove, having first stopped at the natural arch of Durdle Door, cut into the Purbeck limestone. The scenery at Lulworth was the most spectacular in Dorset and Serra gasped now and then as once again they stood together, this time on a grassy rise, looking at one of the most beautiful examples of marine erosion. The surrounding arms of the cove had resisted the pounding of the waves while the softer material inside the cove had been worn away.

'I like this little cove,' she sighed as they sat down on the grass. 'It's exciting seeing new places.'

He turned his head to look at her, watching her lovely face in profile.

'I shall have to arrange for you to drive the car,' he said suddenly. 'Then you can get about on your own if you wish.'

Her eyes clouded as she turned her head.

'You mean——?'

'No, my dear, I don't! I shall continue to take you about, but it would be nice if you could drive the car.'

She smiled then, happily.

'It'll be exciting to drive—but I shall be scared,' she added. 'Will you be teaching me?'

A small, rueful hesitation and then,

'It will probably be advisable to have someone else teach you. I'll ring up a motoring school tomorrow and make the necessary arrangements.'

'You think you'd become impatient with me?'

'I don't think, I'm sure. And impatient is a mild

word. No, Serra, I'm fully aware of the lengths to which my temper will stretch.'

He was in a communicative and approachable mood and Serra felt a sudden surge of happiness. She had told Jenny that she would like to have her husband's company; it had been an automatic statement, but now Serra knew that behind it there had been an odd sense of yearning.

'Do you feel like walking?' Dirk asked after a while.

'Yes, I love walking.'

'Then we'll have a saunter through the woods to East Lulworth.' Here the coast was wild and rough and the waves rolled and leapt with white-foamed fury.

Later, they had tea at a country inn. The atmosphere was medieval, with a large open fireplace at one end of the room and heavy oaken beams crossing the low plastered ceiling.

That evening Dirk's mother came to dine with them; she had of course learned everything from Jenny, and she seemed amused by the whole thing. It would take a great deal to shock Mrs Morgan, Serra concluded, and decided to tell her she had intended calling on her for help.

'I thought you would know what to do with the— the criminal,' she ended with a smile at her mother-in-law.

Both Dirk and his mother laughed.

'I assure you I'm not in the habit of dealing with criminals, Serra,' said Mrs Morgan, her eyes alight with amusement.

'I didn't mean that,' protested Serra. 'I meant that you would have some suggestions. You see, I didn't want Dirk to know what I'd done.'

'That's understandable. Tell me, what happened

when Dirk did come? You didn't describe the scene to Jenny, and I would certainly like to hear about it.'

Lifting her eyes, Serra looked at Dirk. He was amused, and so very different from the scowling husband of the other evening that she could scarcely believe he was the same man. A little surge of pride engulfed her; he was so good-looking, and he had a softened expression which added enormously to his attractiveness as a man.

'Charles had come into my bedroom—Jenny told you that?' And when Mrs Morgan nodded; 'Well, Dirk burst in and thought I was—I mean, Charles was....' She tailed off, going red. Mrs Morgan's shoulders shook, while Dirk was subjecting his wife to a look of mild warning, which she failed to notice because she turned her head as Mrs Morgan spoke.

'How very droll! Just as if Charles would. I'm surprised at you, Dirk. Fancy suspecting your best friend!'

'Mother,' commented Dirk with some asperity, 'that escapade of Serra's was no joking matter! You do realize that the family silver could have been stolen?'

With amazing unconcern Mrs Morgan nodded.

'Perhaps it would have taught you a lesson, Dirk. As Jenny says, you're married and you can't leave your wife to her own devices all the time. Serra must have been very lonely indeed to think of advertising for relatives like that.' She smiled at her daughter-in-law. 'Tell me some more; I find the whole thing most entertaining.'

Serra looked uncertainly at her, and even more uncertainly at Dirk. He was busy with his steak and did not now appear to mind how the conversation went.

'Charles told Dirk why he had come up the fire-escape——'

'He came up the fire-escape? How melodramatic!'

Serra nodded.

'That's what Charles said, but I was trying to keep Preston out of it.'

'Which would be quite impossible. Preston guards this house as if it were his own. To him, everyone is guilty until he is proved innocent. Go on, my dear, we appear to be digressing.'

'There isn't very much else to tell. Charles explained about my advertisement, and then Dirk told us that Roderick had gone.'

'A rather tame ending,' mused Dirk's mother. 'But for the best, probably.'

'Indeed it was for the best. I had a horrid feeling that the police would come and it would all get into the newspapers.'

Dirk glanced up.

'You would have been in trouble then.' His brown eyes held a glint that caused Serra to avert her head. 'It would have been more than a box on the ears.'

Mrs Morgan's eyes widened.

'What did you say?' she demanded.

'You heard me.'

'Jenny said he didn't mean it when he said he'd box my ears,' Serra hurriedly told her mother-in-law, who was looking decidedly disapproving.

'You come and tell me if he lays a finger on you,' said Mrs Morgan, and Dirk grimaced.

'You appear to have champions both in my mother and my sister,' he laughed, his eyes on Serra, who was looking at those little fan-like lines at the corners of his eyes and feeling a strange stirring of some emotion hitherto unknown to her.

'I'm very lucky,' she returned. 'I shan't get into any more trouble now.'

'I sincerely hope you won't, my dear,' from Mrs Morgan, and then, 'What was it about Dirk that made you decide to marry him? There must have been some small attraction other than the prospect of freedom.'

'It was my voice,' commented Dirk, rather lazily. 'She decided she could live with it.'

Serra laughed at her mother-in-law's expression and proceeded to explain about Phivos's voice, which she had heard from the room adjoining that in which the negotiations for her marriage were going on.

'I must agree a voice can be most irritating. As you say, Dirk has a most attractive voice—except of course when he's cross.'

Jenny came over later, having been out all day, shopping in Bournemouth, and the evening passed most pleasantly in talking by the fire in the drawing-room. When at last Jenny and her mother said good night and Serra and Dirk were left alone he stood by the fire, one hand spread along the mantelpiece, and looked at her long and hard.

'You're a nice little thing,' he declared at length, and she glanced swiftly at him, her eyes opening in surprise.

'Thank you,' she returned glowingly. 'I think that means that you're telling me you haven't minded at all being with me today.'

He smiled, and stifled a yawn.

'It's been a most pleasant day,' he said and, a little later when Serra got up from the chair on which she had been sitting, and said good night, Dirk, who had also risen, took her chin in his hand and, regarding her piquant little face for a long moment, he bent his head and kissed her.

'Good night, Serra. Sleep well.'

'Good night,' she said again, shining up at him, a

smile quivering on her lips. 'And thank you ... for today.'

She regarded herself proudly through the mirror. Clad in jodhpurs and a white polo-necked sweater, she looked the elegant young lady, with her finely-contoured classical features touched with peach, and her dark hair, long and straight, falling on to her shoulders.

It was three weeks since Jenny had begun teaching her to ride and as Serra was a confident, apt pupil it was not long before she had almost as much poise and confidence as her sister-in-law. They rode each morning in the park surrounding the Grange, and when it was Dirk's turn to be with Serra she would then ride with him. He praised her on several occasions, bringing rosy blushes to her cheeks, blushes which sometimes brought a smile of amusement to his lips but just as often caused him to frown and become lost in thought, during which he would glance sideways at her and sometimes frown more heavily than ever.

She ran downstairs and Dirk was waiting for her in the hall. His eyes moved over her, slowly and all-embracingly; she felt the colour rise to mantle her cheeks and inclined her head.

'Come,' said Dirk abruptly. 'It looks very much like rain. Let's hope we can get half an hour in before it does.'

The great park was characterized by extensive areas of undulating grassland interspersed with ornamental shrubberies, stately yew hedges with arched entrances, and shady arbours leading off gravel paths which themselves often led on to ornamental pools filled with waterlilies and other aquatic vegetation.

Cantering beside Dirk Serra sent him sidelong

glances whenever she found an opportunity of doing so without his knowledge. His face in profile was hard and finely-chiselled, with a thrusting chin and firm square jaw. There was strength in his face, she thought, and this did not seem to line up with his abandoned way of life. He had this huge estate and many surrounding villages as well. He had work and enough if he required it, so there was no need to seek refuge from boredom in wine and women, as he appeared to do. A fortnight ago he had been on a friend's yacht; it was a lively party, he had told Serra, with lots of beautiful girls. Serra had felt a strange unfamiliar pang as she imagined his being with other girls, making love to them, as of course he would be doing, the same as all his men friends on board the yacht. To Serra it was a strange way to live, and it would appear that there was to be no immediate alteration, for Dirk was off again this week-end on the same yacht, with the same crowd. What a lot of people seemed to have nothing to do but enjoy themselves, she thought, wishing her husband would give it all up and look after his lands and not have a bailiff doing everything as was the case at present.

The clouds were low over the chalk downlands, but the rain kept off and on nearing a pool with a fountain rising from the centre Dirk dismounted. He came to Serra as she jumped to the ground and caught her in his arms. She felt his strength and the warmth of his hands as they slid down to enclose her wrists. In this attitude he stood, looking at her, an odd expression on his face.

'Did anyone ever tell you you were beautiful?' he asked, his eyes kindling as she blushed.

'No. In Greece they don't have the chance to flatter you.'

'Of course. You never have a period of courtship, do you?'

She shook her head.

'I used to imagine I'd have one,' she confessed on a sudden note of shyness. 'That was when Mother was alive. She said I should choose my own husband when I was old enough. She said I would meet someone who would fall in love with me, not someone who just looks at you and likes you as they do in Greece. She used to say that no matter how much Father argued she meant to have her own way over my marriage.' A wistful note crept into her voice; it was a moment of profound quiet, with Dirk still standing close, and holding her wrists in his strong slender hands.

'And you've missed all that.' His tones were gentle and as she looked into his softened face she said impulsively, but earnestly for all that,

'I wouldn't have it any different, Dirk. I'd rather be married to you than to anyone else.'

He gave a little start.

'You don't mind that there'll never be any love in your life?—and no children?'

Silence again. She glanced down to his hands—and all at once she felt tears in her eyes.

'Do you know, I never thought about children.' She turned her head, and gazed wordlessly at the fountain for a long moment. 'I like children very much. We had a lot in the family—with the cousins and aunts and uncles always having babies.'

'Uncles?' But somehow there was no amusement in his voice as the word was uttered.

'You know what I mean.' She produced a smile, but with difficulty. 'No, I never thought about children.'

'You'd like to have some?'

'Yes.' She gave a long trembling sigh and then she

repeated what she had already said.

'I'd rather be married to you than anyone else, though.'

He released her hand, a slight frown creasing his brow.

'I wonder if I've been fair to you,' he murmured, almost to himself. 'It is natural for a woman to have children. And had you been married to Phivos you'd have had several, I expect.'

'I didn't want Phivos, not with a voice like that. No, it doesn't matter about the children——' She broke off, her face brightening as a thought occurred to her. 'Jenny will get married some day and have children; then I'll be an aunt. That'll be better than nothing.'

He frowned again and said.

'You're so satisfied with second best. But will Jen's kids be enough?'

'Of course.' She became thoughtful, looking around at the luxury about her. Then her eyes wandered to the house, and its impressive façade with its Grecian columns topped by an ornate entablature and pediment. 'Don't you want an heir——?' Impulsive the question and she stopped, her cheeks mantling with colour. She dropped her eyes and stepped away from him. There was a seat close by and she moved towards it. He followed, sitting down. The two horses bent to nibble the grass and Dirk's attention appeared to be concentrated on them. Serra turned her head to read his expression, but when he caught her eyes she lowered her head, avoiding his gaze again.

'I expect Jenny's children will inherit,' he began, then stopped. 'Sit down,' he said, patting the place beside him. Serra obeyed, wondering at his strangeness, and the tiny frown line that knit his brow. 'No, he said emphatically, 'I don't want an heir.' He still frowned, but turned to face her. 'It's a little late, in any case, isn't it? There isn't any possibility of my having an heir now that I've married for convenience.'

'No....' But with the passing of time would he become more mature and change his mind? Mature...? She examined his features, as she had examined them many times recently, and saw maturity there, and pride and firmness of character. It was odd that such a man could be satisfied with the life he led. His father had been a rake, according to what Mrs Morgan had said, and so often sons took after their fathers. Dirk wouldn't go as far as his father, Jenny had firmly asserted, and she had also said that she had a feeling her brother would mend his ways quite soon. It would be wonderful, she thought, a glow entering her lovely brown eyes, if Dirk were to become a stay-at-home and they could be together like this all the time. A rueful smile appeared and hovered on her lips as she recalled her previous wish that he would not become a stay-at-home, because she herself wanted to go around and have a good time. Funny, but she no longer wanted a good time—not since Dirk had taken an interest in her.

'How's the driving going?' Dirk spoke into the silence, changing the subject. 'Jenny says you're doing fine.'

'The instructor said so. He said I sit in the car as if I were part of it,' she added, laughing.

'A woman and her car, eh?' His lazy eyes held a hint of humour. 'You'd better be looking round for the kind of car you would like, then I can order it up for you.'

Her eyes widened. He would order a car, he said—just like that! She shone at him, responding like a child who has been praised.

'You're very good to me, Dirk, and I'm really grateful. Oh, I never thought I'd be so lucky as this!'

'We've both been lucky. The marriage is suitable to us and there's no need for gratitude, my dear. I had to be married and——' He broke off, smiling at her with a mingling of apology and amusement. 'No matter what I said, I prefer you to Clarice.'

Again she responded like a child who'd been praised.

'I'm so glad—you have no idea how it's worried me. I felt so inadequate, when I did the wrong things, and you looked so—so scowling and frightening that I was sure you would divorce me and marry Clarice.'

'We don't have divorce in our family,' he told her, then paused in reflection. 'That's why I never wanted to marry. These days the pace and way of life isn't conducive to lasting devotion. One is tempted all the time—girls throw themselves at men, and it doesn't matter that the men might be married. I wanted to be free—so that I could go my own way without hurting anyone.' Again he paused. The horses had strayed towards the pool, then stopped to nibble the grass again. 'But seeing that I had to marry this is ideal. I can do what I like without hurting my wife.'

She was silent, digesting this. He was an honourable man, then, for he did not like hurting people. Her heart warmed to him, and the tiny fluttering of that emotion registered but did not at present impress.

But as they rose from the seat he automatically took hold of her hand, and then it was that she knew a feeling totally new—and exciting. Her heartbeats quickened slightly and her pulse began to act in the strangest way. Dirk walked quickly towards the horses and she trotted to keep up with him. Suddenly he slackened his pace and smiled down at her.

'You're a nice little thing,' he said, repeating the description he had previously used. 'Why didn't you complain?'

'Complain?'

'Tell me I was walking too fast?'

'It didn't matter.' He was still holding her hand; its warmth and strength filled her with a sensation of happiness and well-being; for some reason she remembered that kiss which he had given her on the evening of the first day they had been out together and she was suddenly walking on air. And because of this she did not see that they had to step down from the grass on to a gravel path which the horses had crossed a moment or two ago. With a jerk she came from the grass to the stone edging of the path; she was thrown against Dirk who, with a blank look, caught her as she would have fallen forward.

'What——?'

'I didn't look where I was going....' She was against him, his strong arms encircling her, his eyes looking down into hers. Her own eyes were shy, but bright as stars, her lips quivered and parted a fraction, inviting a kiss. One of the horses whinnied; a gust of wind blew across the park from the west, rustling the leaves and portending a downpour of rain. But neither Dirk nor Serra heard or saw anything except each other, and in the enchantment of the moment he found and held her inviting lips. She trembled against him, kissed like this—with ardour and desire—for the first time in her life.

At last Dirk held her from him, the most odd expression on his face.

'Delightful,' he murmured with the softness of a caress. 'Thoroughly delightful.' And then, in a tone so brusque that it came as a shock, 'The rain—— We'll have to be getting back if we don't want to be soaked to the skin.' And he hurried over to where the horses grazed, not in the least troubled this time that Serra was having to trot to keep pace with him.

CHAPTER EIGHT

A FORTNIGHT later Mrs Morgan gave a dinner party for Jenny's twentieth birthday. It was held on a Saturday, but of course Dirk stayed at home in order to be there. The previous week Jenny had taken Serra to Bournemouth to shop, Jenny sitting beside her as Serra drove her little open sports car, for although Serra had been declared most proficient by her instructor she had not yet taken her test. With her sister-in-law's help Serra had bought a delightful turquoise blue cocktail dress, slim-fitting and short so that every lovely feature and curve of her body was enchantingly highlighted.

Jenny's expression was strange as she regarded Serra, who stood before the mirror in the dressing-room of the shop. She appeared thoughtful, and yet at the same time there was a gleam of satisfaction in her gaze which seemed far in excess of the admiration which also shone from her eyes.

'You'll do very nicely.' A pause and then, 'If Dirk doesn't wake up when he sees you in this, then he never will.'

Serra turned from the mirror.

'What do you mean?' But the mount of colour settling on the high cheekbones gave the lie to Serra's deliberate pretence.

'Don't you want him to fall in love with you?' asked Jenny, half in earnest, half in amusement because of the startled shyness in her sister-in-law's eyes.

'Jenny ... that could never be,' she trembled, making a nervous little pluck at the skirt of her dress. 'He has his own chosen way of life.'

'Many people have a chosen way of life some time or other, but quite often the novelty wears off and they then choose another.'

'You would like Dirk to settle down, wouldn't you?'

'Of course. He is an important squire and landowner; his function is to look to his estate and show an example to his tenants and employees.' Jenny began to unzip Serra's dress. 'I asked if you wanted him to fall in love with you?' she reminded Serra, who paused a long while before answering.

'Yes, Jenny, I would like him to fall in love with me——' Even as she spoke she shook her head. 'He wouldn't—no, he *couldn't* fall in love with anyone like me!' Yet recollection brought back that kiss on the day they were out riding in the park, and she heard her husband's soft and caressing tones as he uttered the word, 'Delightful.' Swift on this delicious memory came the suspicion that Dirk was in the habit of saying that to every girl he kissed, and a shadow fell on Serra's face.

'What's wrong?' demanded Jenny with her customary quick perception. Serra slipped out of the dress and Jenny took it from her. She picked up her skirt and began to put it on.

'He kissed me,' she replied simply, not realizing that this was not an answer to her sister-in-law's question.

'He did?' with sharp interest. 'When?'

'We were out riding, and I nearly fell. He caught me—and—and then kissed me ... nicely,' she added with charming naïveté, and Jenny laughed even though her expression was still one of interest.

'You liked it, obviously?'

Serra gave a shaky laugh then and admitted that she did like it, but went on to add that Dirk had never kissed her since, and she ended by saying,

'I expect I was just another girl.' She took her blouse from the hanger on the wall, watching Jenny's face but not deriving any satisfaction from the hope she saw there. Jenny was far too optimistic, she thought with a tinge of dejection.

'I don't believe that was the reason he kissed you, Serra.' A pause and then, 'You're quite out of the ordinary run of girls he associates with. In fact, were I in his position I'm sure I'd find you most refreshing.'

'Out of the run?' Serra tried to retain some sort of composure under this outspoken flattery.

'I don't expect he's had much experience of innocent girls,' Jenny murmured, watching Serra as she buttoned up her blouse. 'And I'm very sure you're quite the most beautiful girl he's ever known.'

'Jenny...! You can't mean that!'

'I wouldn't have said it if I hadn't meant it.'

No more was said because the assistant appeared and Jenny handed her the dress. On the way home the two girls stopped at a restaurant for afternoon tea, and that evening, as Dirk was away from home, Serra dined at the Dower House. She was happy, but the new emotion which had germinated troubled her a little. Supposing she were to fall madly in love with her husband...? Already it hurt when she thought about his being with other girls ... and she suspected that very soon that hurt would increase to sheer agony.

Many people attending the dinner party regarded Serra curiously on being introduced to her, and their eyes would invariably stray—amusement in their depths—to her husband, whose reputation was no secret. It was also widely known that his father, although a rake himself for practically the whole of his life, had at the end decided he did not want his son to follow the same path, and that the will was made with the object of putting a halt to Dirk's carefree life. It was also common knowledge that the old man's objective had failed, hence the amusement. No one felt sorry for Serra, though, it being generally accepted that she had done very well for herself.

It was Jenny who introduced Serra to Clarice, who instantly revealed the animosity she felt. It was reflected back from the hard blue eyes and the sudden tightening of Clarice's lips on hearing Serra's name.

'Do you mind if I leave you?' Jenny smiled at her sister-in-law as she made a gesture towards another new arrival. 'I'll be back directly.'

Serra and Clarice were sitting on a couch, in a lighted alcove at one end of the drawing-room; an impassive black-suited manservant was serving drinks to the guests, who all sat around, chatting. Serra had been thrilled with the merry atmosphere and the new people to whom she was introduced, but now she felt flat and inadequate because of Clarice's poise and the air of glamour that seemed to emanate from her. She was very fair-skinned with pale gold hair put up in an elegant coiffure which in itself spelled confidence. Even Serra's lovely dress seemed indistinctive beside the model of perfection her companion wore.

'I congratulate you on your marriage.' Clarice's low smooth voice was devoid of sincerity. 'Dirk was the catch of the season.'

'The——?' Serra had never heard the expression; it sounded most indelicate and she frowned. 'What is that?'

A laugh that was almost a sneer issued from Clarice's lips. She ignored Serra's question as she asked,

'What part of Greece do you come from? One of the small, backward villages?'

Serra's pointed little chin lifted; across the room she

caught her husband's eye. He smiled as if amused at seeing her sitting there, with the girl who had expected to marry him.

'My home was in Athens—the capital,' she added with emphasis.

'Odd how people rave about that city,' Clarice drawled, digressing a little, and without reason, Serra thought. 'I couldn't abide it!'

'It appeals mainly to people with aesthetic tastes,' came the swift riposte, and Clarice's face darkened.

'Your lack of diplomacy amounts to rudeness,' she snapped. Then that makes two of us, Serra thought, for Clarice's remarks had certainly been rude. But Serra felt she could understand how the girl felt. Everyone expecting Dirk to marry her—it must not only have been disappointing to discover he was married, but humiliating as well. Clarice was speaking again, this time in a more subdued tone. 'How long have you known Dirk? None of us was aware he had friends in Greece.'

A moment's reflective silence. Serra was tempted to come out with the truth, saying she and Dirk had picked each other up on the Acropolis, just for the amusement of seeing Clarice's reaction. But Serra again caught her husband's eye and she refrained. He would not wish her to be so outspoken as that.

'We didn't know each other very long,' she answered, looking about for Jenny.

'How long? Was it merely a holiday—er—romance?' The sarcasm was so pointed that a flush of anger rose to Serra's cheeks. And the next moment Dirk had joined them, his eyes warning as he sat down on a chair facing his wife. He must have known that the position was dangerous, she surmised, and had decided to intrude before Serra once again allowed her impulsiveness to run away with her.

'Dirk,' murmured Clarice silkily, 'I wondered when you were going to remember your manners and come over to me.'

His brows shot up.

'It's Mother's party,' he reminded her smoothly. 'It is not incumbent on me to move round the guests.' He beckoned negligently and a moment later a drink was placed before him. 'You, Clarice—another drink?'

Her eyes were glinting at his snub, but she managed a smile as she told him what she wanted.

'I've just been asking Serra how long you knew one another.' Her smile deepened; it would appear that she had no intention of antagonizing him. 'She was evasive.'

'It was a whirlwind romance.' His steady gaze met Clarice's and she held it, challengingly.

'How exciting,' she murmured in some amusement. 'You swept Serra off her feet, apparently.'

Again Serra's chin went up. Before Dirk knew what she had in mind her words tumbled out.

'Everyone knows why Dirk married me, so the pretence is unnecessary!' And she added, despite the awful look she received from her husband, 'If you two want to discuss the marriage then I'll leave you to do it unhindered by my presence.' With great dignity she rose from the couch. 'If you'll excuse me...?' And with even greater dignity she moved away, her emotions a mingling of anger, hurt and apprehension, for of a certainty Dirk would scold her later, when the opportunity arose.

'What's to do?' Jenny came up to Serra just as the dinner gong sounded. 'You look flustered. Clarice?' she ended briefly.

'I've done it again,' confessed Serra unhappily.

'Done what?'

'Something wrong—and undignified. I told Dirk and Clarice that if they wanted to discuss the marriage then they could do it in private. And I left them to it.'

Jenny frowned uncomprehendingly and Serra explained.

'You idiot! Never mind, though. Clarice asked for it, obviously.'

'You don't think it was very dreadful of me?'

'Of course I do,' and after the merest pause, 'But as I'd have done the same myself I can't very well express disapproval.'

Dirk sat opposite to his wife at the dinner table, which was laid with the finest silver and Sèvres porcelain and lit by silver-gilt candelabra and small individual lights in the form of silver lanterns distributed along both sides of the massive table.

For the most part, Serra avoided his glances, but now and then he would manage to catch her eye and on those occasions he gave her the sort of warning glance that told her clearly she was in for a reprimand.

Jenny, sitting on her mother's right, was not ignorant of what was going on and she sent her sister-in-law compensating glances which put heart into Serra and she smiled gratefully.

Later, there was dancing in the brilliantly-lighted ballroom and Dirk immediately invited Clarice to dance with him.

'Take no notice,' advised Jenny. 'He's only paying you out; he doesn't give a toss for Clarice.'

Nevertheless, for over an hour he gave Clarice his undivided attention and Serra became sunk in misery and humiliation as she noticed the glances that were cast at her. So when she danced with the handsome

Bernard Hinde she laughed a lot and, in fact, flirted with him, and when he suggested they go out on to the terrace she willingly agreed, noticing with satisfaction that Dirk was watching them as he danced with his glamorous partner.

'You're a beauty,' flattered Bernard who, though Serra did not know it, was a notorious flirt. 'How did Dirk come by such a fortune?' They had found a seat where they were out of sight of the people in the ballroom and Bernard gestured for Serra to sit down. 'He doesn't appreciate his luck, that's for sure.'

She was shy, already regretting having come out with this young man who, she suspected, was not in the least sincere.

'I don't know what you mean.' She edged away because he had come too close.

'He should take more care of you. Why, he's always off somewhere. He'll regret it when you start playing the same game. Clarice, in there—he's never taken his eyes off her all evening.' Bernard moved closer and she flinched as she felt his breath on her face. 'Kiss me, my lovely Grecian beauty——' Before Serra knew what was happening he had her in his arms and she was struggling vainly to free herself.

'Let me go! Leave me alone!' But he smothered her protest with kisses and did not desist until he himself was breathless.

'How dare you!' She stood up and stamped her foot. 'My husband——'

'Won't do a thing, my dear.' He was on his feet and she tried to run, her cheeks flaming, her hand brushing her mouth in her endeavour to erase the still-present feel of his kisses. He grabbed her arm and swung her into his embrace. 'Shy and timid—but how refreshing. I'll teach you to love, if you'll let me——'

'Love? I hate you! Let me go or I'll shout for help!'

'No such thing. You flirted with me in there, and although you're shy now you'll not be for long——' He broke off, releasing her as a shadow fell across the terrace.

'All right,' said Jenny in a furious tone. 'Cut it out, Bernard. Serra's not your kind of girl. Serra, come on!'

'Oh, Jenny,' Serra breathed a moment later when they were in a small private parlour used only by Jenny and her mother. 'I'm so glad you came.' She brushed a hand through her hair. 'What was the matter with him?'

Despite the censure in her eyes Jenny had to laugh.

'Really! Serra, you're not safe to be let loose. What do you expect was the matter with him?'

'But he knows I'm married,' protested Serra, rubbing her mouth again and frowning in acute distaste because even now she could feel those vile kisses. 'He didn't seem to be afraid Dirk would come out and catch him kissing me.'

'Perhaps he thought Dirk didn't notice you leave the ballroom, but he did; another moment and he would have been out. I felt it best to rescue you because Dirk's temper's so unpredictable and I didn't want a brawl taking place out there, not on my birthday.'

Serra stared, because Jenny was so cool now and there was no mistaking the laughter in her eyes.

'I flirted with him, didn't I?' Serra looked hopefully at Jenny, inviting a denial.

'I didn't happen to see you, but I heard Bernard saying you did. You don't even smile invitingly at a man like him, let alone flirt. He's a pompous ass who believes he's irresistible to women. I only invited him because his sister's a great friend of mine—Janice, you were sitting by her at dinner.'

Serra nodded, remembering that she had liked Janice, who had chatted and been most sincere in her congratulations.

'Thank you for rescuing me.' Serra gave Jenny a look of gratitude before adding, 'I suppose you consider me very silly?'

'Not at all. You're just too innocent for this sort of set-up. You'll have to learn to discriminate, to be far less trusting than you are.'

'In Greece we trust everybody,' Serra commented rather sadly.

'You mean, a man wouldn't try to kiss you?'

Serra looked horrified.

'Never! You see, they all want to marry good girls, so they respect us.'

Jenny did not seem able to accept that.

'The male of the species is the same the world over.'

'Greek men do have—er—friends,' conceded Serra. 'But they are usually women who don't want to marry —in fact, they scarcely ever do marry.'

'It still seems unbelievable that a man wouldn't make a pass at you if the chance came his way.'

Chance never came the way of the boys, Serra explained. The girls were too well protected by their fathers and brothers. Jenny shrugged and changed the subject, asking if Serra were sufficiently collected to return to the ballroom.

Serra nodded, and thanked Jenny again for rescuing her.

'I'm not quite sure I did the right thing,' mused Jenny, making a half-turn towards the door. 'Perhaps I should have allowed nature to take its course, as it were. It would have been interesting to see how Dirk would react to the spectacle of his wife in another man's arms——'

'He would have been very angry,' broke in Serra with haste. 'No, Jenny, you did right in coming to find me before he did.'

'I'm still not sure.' Jenny fell silent, pondering. 'That he would have been angry is certain——' a pause and then Jenny said softly, as if she did not care whether Serra heard or not, 'It would have been enlightening to know just why he would have been angry?'

Serra frowned.

'Because he's my husband, and he'd feel humiliated.'

'Humiliated? My dear Serra, Dirk has never in his whole life experienced humiliation.' Another pause. 'I *should* have let things take their course. However,' she added briskly, 'I didn't, so there's no use wasting time in regrets. You're fully recovered from your encounter with the Don Juan of Portford Magna?'

Serra had to laugh as she nodded an affirmative. Her laugh was soft and silver-edged, like pixie music floating from a magic reed. But it ended on a little quaver, for Dirk was standing in the doorway, having silently pushed the door open. Serra swallowed, but Jenny sent him a calm smile and invited him to come in. His brown eyes glinted. Never had Serra seen such a harsh and frightening expression on his face as he said smoulderingly to Jenny,

'So you beat me to it, eh? What did you surprise? Tell me, if you please!'

'Surprise?' Jenny blinked at him. How small she appeared beside him, thought Serra, whose heart was beating overrate and her throat felt tight because of the little grip of apprehension clinging there.

'What were they doing when you went out to them?' He spoke to Jenny, but his dark intimidating gaze was fixed on his wife's pallid face.

'Are you referring to Bernard and Serra?' inquired Jenny with a lift of her brow.

His teeth gritted at the evasion. He looked quite capable of boxing Jenny's ears, thought Serra, taking a sudden step backwards as Dirk advanced into the middle of the room.

'What were you and Bernard doing out there?' demanded Dirk, now putting the question to his wife.

She gave a nervous little cough, her eyes darting to Jenny as if she would have her sister-in-law provide her with some clue as to how she must answer this question. The silent inquiry did not go unobserved by Dirk and dark fury edged his tone as he snapped,

'Answer me!—at once!'

Another nervous cough and then, impelled by the demands of honesty, Serra murmured, hanging her head,

'He kissed me.'

An awful silence followed the brief admission. Jenny sent her brother a surreptitious glance from under her lashes; she seemed glad that Serra had told the truth.

'He kissed you, did he?' Vibrating tones with fury caught in the emphasis of every word.

'I didn't want him to.' Serra still kept her head averted, feeling Dirk had a right to be angry, yet at the same time puzzled that his anger should be so strong. It wasn't as if he really cared that someone kissed her, he just didn't like the idea, that was all. 'I felt sick.'

For a moment he seemed speechless; Serra felt she would have been quite terrified had not her sister-in-law been present. Ignoring her second sentence he said,

'So you didn't want him to, eh?' Another step brought him close to Serra, who again stepped back.

'Why, then, were you flirting with him in the ballroom?'

'She wasn't flirting,' put in Jenny. 'How can you accuse Serra of such a thing?'

His eyes glinted as he glanced at Jenny.

'She wasn't? Then how came he to invite her on to the terrace?' Jenny made no answer and Dirk added, 'You know full well she was flirting. Every damned guest in the room knew it!'

'Is that why you're so angry?' asked Serra on a note of apology. 'I expect people would think it odd that I should flirt with someone else, but after all,' she added, trying to melt him with a smile, 'they all know why we married, and as you were flirting with Clarice——'

'I was not flirting with Clarice!'

'Well, it certainly looked like flirting to me. Even Bernard passed remarks about your not taking your eyes off her the whole evening,' she ended without thinking.

'So you were discussing me—in between your more amorous indulgences!' He looked likely to explode and Jenny watched him shrewdly, deliberately keeping out of the conversation for the present.

'Amorous?' the word was new to Serra and she looked questioningly at him. His swift intake of breath was like an animal hiss and her expression changed to one of innocence. What was the matter with him? 'You did say I could do as I liked,' she thought to remind him. But the reminder had no effect; he had not absorbed it, she felt sure, because his glowering expression remained.

'When I said that I had no idea what I was in for!' Serra had no comment to make, merely bowing her head again. 'You, if you remember,' her husband went on, 'promised to give me no trouble!'

She raised her eyes then, and they were wide and contrite and Dirk's gaze became fixed on her, examining every lovely line of her face with a sort of compulsive interest. She looked so young and so lacking in armour. Watching them both for a second or two Jenny gave a satisfied little smile. Then she said briskly,

'Shall we get back to the ballroom? Mother will be wondering if anything's wrong, with us all being absent, that is.'

Her brother was still intently observing his wife, his anger rapidly decreasing until a mere dying spark remained. As Charles had advised, he had acquired a sense of humour, and there could be no retention of his fury while Serra stood there, small and contrite and yet with a look of puzzlement in her big brown eyes because she obviously considered her 'crime' undeserving of such wrath.

'Yes, we'll go back.' The merest pause and then, 'You, my girl, will dance with me for the rest of the evening. I'll keep you out of mischief somehow!'

Mrs Morgan had obviously been looking round for them because she smiled and her expression was one of relief when they all re-entered the ballroom. Dirk danced with Serra and then they sat down at the table where Mrs Morgan was seated.

Was something wrong? she wanted to know, with a swift glance at Dirk before her gaze settled on Serra.

Serra shook her head, then stopped, sending an inquiring look at her husband.

'Spill it if you want to,' he nodded with resignation.

'I don't think you want me to,' she murmured, at which Dirk sighed, then laughed.

'She's been outside on the terrace with Bernard,' he told his mother. 'Jenny knows all about it, so I can't see the reason for this reluctance on Serra's part. You'll hear it all before the night's out. If I've done nothing else I've provided my family with some amusement by my marriage!'

Colour mounted Serra's cheeks, but for some reason she was feeling exceedingly happy and free from the dejection which had enveloped her while Dirk was giving all his attention to Clarice.

'Why did you do that?' Mrs Morgan looked interrogatingly at her daughter-in-law. 'What were you doing out there with Bernard?'

Serra swallowed hard, unable to answer.

'Allowing him to kiss her,' obliged Dirk, but this time he did not laugh. 'She has no sense at all.'

'I didn't think he would kiss me,' protested Serra flashing him an indignant glance. 'He seemed quite nice until then—except he flattered me,' she added as a frowning afterthought.

'Didn't you like that?' Dirk asked, his voice faintly crisp.

'It wasn't sincere.'

'So ... you did gather that much?' She nodded and he went on, 'Why, then, didn't you come back inside?'

'He was kissing me before I could even think,' she began. 'He's stupid!'

Dirk laughed, but his mother shook her head unbelievingly.

'Serra, most girls would have loved to have Bernard kiss them.'

'And gone all willowy and sighed for more,' put in Dirk, adding, 'But all he did for Serra was to make her want to vomit,' and he continued, despite the visible shudder which his disapproving parent gave, 'Serra has a certain weakness there. She feels sick for the most curious reasons.'

'You're laughing at me,' she accused, but her face glowed and she bestowed a happy smile upon him.

A muscle moved in his throat; he looked older, somehow, and more mature.

'Let's dance,' he said abruptly, and rose from his chair.

CHAPTER NINE

WHEN they got home Dirk wanted to know what she had been saying to Clarice.

'You were downright rude at the end,' he admonished before she could reply to his question.

'She asked for it!'

'Why—what did she say to you?' he inquired curiously.

'She said I had made the catch of the season—at least, she said you were the catch of the season.'

Amusement kindled in Dirk's eyes.

'You should have been gratified.'

'I didn't really know what it meant.'

'Did you tell Clarice you didn't?' Dirk leant back in his big armchair and regarded his wife through half closed eyes.

'I gave her to understand that I didn't, and she then asked me if I came from a backward village.' The recollection brought a sparkle to Serra's eyes and Dirk's lips quivered.

'So you proudly told her you came from Athens?'

'Yes. And she said she didn't like Athens——' Serra looked challengingly at her husband before adding, 'I said it appeals mainly to people with aesthetic tastes. That riled her, and I was glad!'

'You can be quite bitchy when you like.' He spoke musingly, his gaze examining yet humorous. 'What had she to say to that?'

'She told me I was rude, but I didn't retaliate,' she added with a sudden hint of regret.

'I'm amazed.

'She then asked how long I'd known you.' Serra laughed suddenly and her eyes twinkled. 'I felt like telling her that we'd picked each other up on the Acropolis and that I'd had to run off to be si——'

'But you didn't inform her of these things,' he interrupted hastily. 'You surprise me.'

'I thought you'd be cross, otherwise I would have done.'

'I'm glad you practised some small amount of restraint.' He regarded her inscrutably but, somehow, she felt he had a reason for what he had just said.

'I was just about to say something scathing, though,' Serra admitted imperturbably. 'But you came along and I didn't have the chance.'

'Once again, I'm glad your tongue was curbed.'

He yawned and glanced at the clock.

'Yes,' Serra smiled. 'It's time we were going to bed. Oh, but I've enjoyed myself tonight.' She stood up, a lovely dainty figure with all the noble Grecian lines of a classical sculpture. 'Especially the last part,' she murmured dreamily. 'When you danced with me all the time, that was.' His warmth against her body, the rhythmic movements that set a nerve tingling, then a pulse, and then her whole being had become affected by the nearness of him. New emotions, vivid and exciting; quiverings and tremors and strange yearnings that teased, because as yet they were vague and indefinable.

'You enjoyed dancing with me?' He spoke softly, rising from his chair as he did so. 'It was supposed to be a punishment—and a restriction on any further flirtations you might have decided to indulge in.'

She twinkled at him, then fluttered her lashes. His lids came down so that his eyes were half closed, yet perception was there ... and another expression that sent her heart racing. Did Dirk like her?

'You know very well I wouldn't have flirted again,' she protested. 'And I never shall.'

A small profound silence and then, with gentle humour,

'You'll never flirt again, you say?' No answer, just a tint of colour rising because Serra had caught his meaning and she knew she had not been very clever. So it came as no surprise when he added, still in those soft and humorous tones, 'What, then, are you doing at present?'

'I—I——' Swift colour now, rising rapidly; she half turned from him, but his arms came about her and she was soon facing him, looking up into laughing brown eyes—the eyes of a rake, and yet.... Hadn't she seen a new maturity in those eyes earlier tonight? It was there at this profound moment, strong and steady, and permanent, she thought, her swift-winged memory reverting to Jenny and her confident assertion that it would not be long before he mended his ways. Then Serra's thought switched for one fleeting moment to her own intention of having a good time once she got to England. Now, she had no wish to have a good time—at least, not in the way she had pictured. All she wanted was to be with her husband, whether it be attending dinner parties, riding in the park, or just sitting with him quietly in the house.

'Weren't you flirting with me?' Soft words and the caress of clean cool breath on her forehead. 'You were, you know....' His lips found hers in a long kiss, gentle and warm. She quivered like some frightened bird caught and held, yet not trapped.

'No ... no, I don't th-think s-so,' she managed when at last he gave her the opportunity of speaking.

A soft laugh was his only response; he still held her, in a possessive manner, and as they stood there in the elegant room, so quiet except for the muted tick of the French marble clock, Serra experienced that inevitable access of revelation. She knew she loved her husband, and the wonder of it became reflected in her eyes. Her mother had told her about love, but Serra had resigned herself to the fact that she would never know its meaning, for despite her efforts at defiance she felt that one day she must succumb to pressure and marry a man whom her father chose for her. That, or spinsterhood, she had decided. And now.... But Dirk did not return her love. He divided his attention among several women, it seemed, none of whom meant anything more to him than the physical pleasure their charms could provide.

'It's late,' she murmured awkwardly at length. 'Past one o'clock.'

'We can lie in tomorrow.' His lips were a sigh and a dream away from hers; she willed him to kiss her. 'I shan't be going out tomorrow, so there's nothing for me to get up early for.'

She stared in disbelief.

'You always go out on Sundays—I mean, you usually go off for the week-end.'

'I couldn't this week-end, could I?'

'No, but you could go off tomorrow.'

'Perhaps, but I'm not going to.'

'Jenny's coming to take me fossil-hunting,' she said breathlessly, and at that he frowned.

'That girl's crazy about fossils!'

'This is the best place in England for them.'

'One of the best places,' he corrected, though absently. 'Oh, well, we'll all go fossil-hunting.'

Her whole body quivered against him.

'You—as well? You really want to come with us?'

'What time are you starting out?' he inquired

guardedly before answering her question.

'Not until after lunch. Jenny said she'd be tired too, and wants a lie-in tomorrow morning.'

'Very well, then I shall come with you.' Another silence. She saw the slight movement of his mouth, as if some emotion had caught him also. 'Good night, little girl,' he said softly—and her swift, sudden drift of hope was swept away.

'Good night, Dirk.' Again she invited his kiss. He smiled at her and, reaching the door, held it for her to pass before him. Together they went upstairs.

Serra's bedroom door was reached before Dirk's, whose was the next one along the wide, picture-lined corridor. He stood a moment, looking into the room after she had swung the door inwards. The great tester bed was hung with gold and net drapes; a pelmet of ruched gold satin was fluted into scallops between which hung long gold tassels. The bedcovers were turned down; Serra's filmy nightdress had been draped prettily by her maid, and it lay over one white pillow, seductive in its transparency and subtle contrast of colour, for it was made up of several shades of rose, diminishing in strength until, at the top, the colour was no more than a subtle shade of peach. Dirk's eyes flickered from the bed to the lovely girl who was his wife—the girl he had chosen so that he would never even know he was married. She shone up at him, her eyes soft and trusting as a fawn's. She saw him swallow hard, and something urged her to keep her sleepy lids from drooping. She blinked rapidly in an effort to do so and yet her lids did droop in spite of this. A smile curved her husband's mouth; he ruffled her hair and said,

'Good night—my little girl. Sleep well.' A light kiss was dropped on each tired lid and a moment later he was at his own bedroom door. A lean brown hand was raised in salute and then both he and Serra had disappeared into their own rooms, and the doors were softly closed. Serra stood with her back to hers, resting against it. So this was love. This sweet and precious thing, this warmth, this ecstasy. Would Dirk come to love her? She laughed softly to herself ... and remembered how, at first, she would very much have preferred Charles as a husband.

'Thank you, dear Mary, for not letting it be Charles,' she whispered devoutly, and began to undress.

Dirk drove the car and they made for Lyme Regis where, after finding a place to park close to the beach, they left the car and began walking in the direction of Pinhay Bay. The two girls wore slacks and shirts and carried geological hammers. Rucksacks were swung on their backs. Dirk also wore a pair of old slacks and an open-necked shirt. All wore strong boots, Serra having been into Weymouth the previous morning to buy hers.

Jenny had naturally expressed surprise when her brother was waiting, all ready to accompany them on their fossil-hunting expedition. Her lashes shaded her expression and she merely expressed the minimum of surprise necessary to the unusual behaviour of her brother. But her eyes strayed from him to Serra and as on several other occasions she allowed herself a satisfied little smile.

'Can we start now?' Serra wanted to know. She had seen Jenny's wonderful fossil collection and she was eager to begin finding some fossils of her own. One could buy them, of course, but that sort of collecting was for amateurs, not geologists, Jenny had told Serra, who had promptly reminded her that she herself was only an amateur.

'You'll not be one for long. If the bug gets you as it got me then you'll soon be wanting to know more about the rocks and the wonderful treasures one can find in them.'

'We don't start now,' Dirk replied before Jenny could do so. 'Jen likes to go to the farthest point first and then work back—which is sensible, of course, because of the weight one has to carry.'

'Have you been with Jenny before?' Serra glanced at her husband in some surprise. He smiled at her expression and nodded.

'We used to do a lot at one time.' He glanced at his sister, then away again. Jenny said nothing; Serra wondered if she were thinking of those days, which must have been happy ones for both brother and sister, because of their being close, as Charles had said they were. Now, Jenny was probably thinking, Dirk had other pursuits with which to occupy his time.

'Have you a collection, then?' Serra inquired of her husband, who instantly shook his head.

'No, Serra; Jenny has all we collected.'

They walked and talked until they reached the part of the cliffs which were formed of what geologists called the Blue Lias, which were beds consisting of alternations of limestone and shale.

'Here's where we begin looking?' Dirk glanced questioningly at Jenny. 'Okay?'

She nodded, smiling.

'See what you can find, Serra—here, in the shales.'

The other two stood back and watched. Eagerly Serra walked along, looking carefully, but finding nothing and feeling more and more disappointed as the moments passed. At last she turned, retracing her steps.

'There isn't a thing,' she told them in a flat voice. They looked at one another and laughed.

'You have to get your eye in, my dear,' said Dirk with his lazy drawl suddenly in evidence. 'Come, I'll show you.'

It was like a magician at a party, she thought as, with a deft movement of those long fingers, Dirk would extract one after another of the Lamellibranchs abounding in the shale.

'This little fellow's called *Avicula*,' he informed Serra, standing close in order to show her the shell— now cast in stone—he held in his hand. 'There are sub-species, of course, and I think this is——' He paused, looking at Jenny. '*Pteria contorta?*' Jenny nodded, but her eyes were not on the fossil. They were on Serra, who was obviously very conscious of Dirk's nearness because she also, for the moment, was not all that interested in the fossil. 'Are you paying attention?' he said sharply, and Serra did then bend her head to examine the tiny animal that had lived over a hundred and fifty million years ago.

They then all three began to search, and Serra gradually managed to 'get her eye in' and several times the shore would ring with her call of excitement when she had found something. Often, she would be unable to remove the fossil from the rock and then the hammer and chisel would be brought into use. This extraction, without breaking the fossil, was an art acquired only with practice and Serra broke several shells before deciding to let one of the others do it for her.

'You'll soon learn,' Dirk told her, smiling at her self-deprecating shrug as she again handed over her small chisel to him. 'You can't expect to become proficient on your first hunt. This is quite a specialised thing. One learns slowly, so you must have patience. There— you have a little beauty.'

They moved on, under a clear blue sky from which streamed down brilliant sunshine. The beaches were busy with sunbathers, but not crowded. The fossil-hunters attracted a little attention, but they and their like were a familiar sight in this, one of the most productive areas in the whole of the country.

The Blue Lias was packed with *echinoderm* spines, and also contained oyster beds from which Serra added several *Ostrea* to her collection. But of course it was the *ammonites* she was really waiting for and at last they reached the part of the cliff which yielded these up.

They had brought a picnic lunch and Jenny suggested they take a rest and have their sandwiches and coffee before doing any more 'hunting'.

'A good idea.' Dirk had brought a lightweight groundsheet in his rucksack and this he spread on the shore, then he lay down while the two girls took out the flasks and sandwiches and paper plates and beakers.

'This is a very pleasant way of spending a Sunday!' A happy smile was bestowed first on Jenny and then on Dirk. 'I'm very grateful to you both for bringing me.'

'Don't talk as if we've done you a favour,' said Jenny with a slight frown. 'I love fossil-hunting, and so does Dirk, even if he's given it a rest for some time.'

He nodded, although amusement flecked his dark eyes at his sister's rather pointed remark.

'I did used to enjoy it immensely,' he owned, sitting up as Serra held out his coffee to him. 'And I do believe today's whetted my appetite again. We must repeat this some time.'

'Some time?' Jenny handed him a plate, and with the other hand offered him sandwiches.

'Next Sunday, if you like?' he murmured, watching her for any sign of satisfaction she might register. Jenny was far too clever. Her brother was stubborn ... and the change in him which she so fervently desired was only just beginning. She must not display triumph yet—not until her brother's surrender was a little more advanced.

'Next Sunday?' quivered Serra, her face glowing. 'Aren't you going away for the week-end?'

His lazy eyes flickered over her face; he saw the dimples—reflections of an inner happiness—and the clear shining eyes, demurely veiled now and then by the enchanting screen of long curling lashes.

'No,' he returned softly. 'I'm not going away for the week-end——' He caught his sister's eye and she instantly glanced away. It was difficult not to reveal her satisfaction and she feared she had not been sufficiently cautious this time even before her brother said, 'A penny for your thoughts, Jen.'

She shrugged and thrust the plate of sandwiches forward so that he could not ignore them.

'Thoughts are secrets, my inquisitive brother!'

He took a sandwich, his eyes never leaving her face.

'Thoughts are things with airy wings; they're often imprudent, though, and can easily be caught.'

'Have you caught mine?' she challenged, admitting there was nothing to be gained by further prevarication.

'Without the slightest trouble.' His eyes glinted. 'You won't reform me,' he said in clipped and even tones. 'I told you that once before.'

'I might not, but....' Significantly she allowed her

voice to trail away, at the same time glancing at her sister-in-law, who was absorbed in cutting up tomatoes and putting them on a plate.

'No one,' he said slowly and emphatically on noting the direction of his sister's eyes, 'will reform me.'

Lifting her face, Serra looked at him; he met her gaze and she saw a hardness there, a hardness like the flint that abounded everywhere, brought down from the undulating chalk hills of Dorset. She swallowed and lowered her eyes, and for a few moments she just stared at the plate in her hand, then she held it out to Dirk.

'I'll give you a fork,' she offered on realizing he was looking around for something with which to pick up the tomatoes she was giving to him.

'Thank you.' Their fingers touched, and Serra felt needle points behind her eyes because his touch hurt now and she wanted to cry. He was saying he would never change, saying that he would always be a rake ... and yet she loved him, loved him so that her heart was wounded by his words and by the hardness in his gaze.

Yet with her usual resiliency she managed to shake off her hurt and displayed as much excitement as ever when, a short while later, she found her first 'snake stone' which was an *ammonite* of high quality and of quite a large size. She later found a couple of *Gryphoea*, and then a specimen of what the locals called a tortoise *ammonite*, which had its chambers filled with pure white calcite.

'Is it something very rare?' she wanted to know, holding it as if it were a piece of rare Chelsea porcelain.

'Not really—sorry,' laughed Jenny on seeing her face fall. 'There isn't anything new around here, I'm afraid.'

'Unless Serra finds a fossilized skeleton of a reptile—Ichthyosaur, for instance,' put in Dirk, also laughing.

'That isn't new,' Jenny pointed out. 'They're found mainly in the Lias.'

'But it would be a rare find for a private collector.'

'And difficult to extract.' She turned to Serra, who was wrapping her latest find in a piece of newspaper. 'They're often about two foot long.'

'I might find one some day,' returned Serra hopefully, taking out a piece of string and securing her parcel. Then she filled in a label and tied it to the string.

'All very methodical,' teased Dirk, watching the precious find go into Serra's rucksack.

'I want to know where I found it, and on what date.' She looked across at him as she said this, and he read the message in her eyes. This, for Serra was a very special date.

The sun was setting when at last they arrived back at the Grange, and down below the sea was a quivering carpet of crimson as the molten sky became reflected in it. On the green hills amber sprayed the pastures as the descending orb of fire spread its translucent glory across the tranquil, drowsy landscape. Sheep on the hillsides were clothed in dappled bronze. The church, built of lovely Purbeck marble and already weathered to a unique tawny-brown, was enriched with pure gold ochre so that it appeared as a shining sentinel, standing high on a knoll above the sleepy village of Portford Magna.

'Gosh,' exclaimed Jenny, 'I'm tired!' Her car was on the forecourt where she had left it on her arrival at the Grange. Dirk glanced at her as she got out of his car and asked if she would like him to drive her home.

'You can collect your car tomorrow,' he suggested. 'It'll be all right here for tonight.'

'Thanks, Dirk, but I'll not trouble you. It's only a couple of minutes' drive.' She walked over to her own car and slid into the driver's seat. "Bye, you two. See you soon,' and she was gone, switching on her lights only when she had entered the area of the park that ran through the grove of ancient spreading oak trees.

Serra and Dirk dined alone and afterwards sat in the cosy room and drank coffee and talked. But there was a subtle change in Dirk; he was harder, somehow; less approachable. He reminded her of the man she had first met, and when she went to bed that night she did not laugh softly to herself, for her heart had mislaid its lightness. Somehow, through no fault of her own, she had lost ground.

She turned her face into the pillow, determined not to cry.

'Mary,' she whispered on a note of frantic urgency, 'please make him love me.'

CHAPTER TEN

As the days passed it seemed to Serra that Dirk became more and more distant and she at last began to wonder if he now regretted his hasty marriage to her. He had said at the time that he'd no intention of being restricted in any way, but he was now being restricted and it would appear that this restriction was becoming irksome.

There seemed to be only one way of freeing him, and that was for Serra to go home for a while. Dirk had promised her that she could pay a visit to her father, so he would not consider it strange if she suggested it just now. While she was away he would revert to his old life of complete freedom, and on her return she would suggest he carried on as usual. Jenny would be angry, but Serra did not think she herself would go back on her word and follow Dirk's example, leaving Serra once again to her own devices. Yes, Serra decided one morning when she and Dirk were having breakfast together, she would go home for a time. Much better to let Dirk indulge in his old way of life than that he should come to consider his marriage a burden, and his wife an encumbrance.

She looked at him across the table, intent on broaching the subject at once, but he was so preoccupied, and his brow was knit in a frown, and she decided to wait until another time.

'Where are we going today?' he asked at last, and she flinched at his brusque tone.

'If you want to—to stay in,' she began when he interrupted her with,

'You said you'd like to go swimming. We could go today.'

'Yes, all right.' She toyed with her toast but presently pushed it aside. Now that she had finally made up her mind to go home she felt choked, and shot through with misery.

Serra drove her own little car, at Dirk's suggestion, and although she felt nervous, it being the first time she had driven him, she managed to do quite nicely and to her relief he had no faults to find with her driving. In fact he said, when she drew on to the car park above the beach,

'You're quite the little expert. You should pass your test first time.'

She glowed for a moment and smiled up at him as he stood beside her, watching her lock the car door.

To her surprise Dirk's ill-humour soon dissolved as they swam together in the clear blue water, and he even teased her a little, saying she must be shivering after having been used to the warm waters of Greece.

'Did you go swimming much?' he then asked, and she nodded. They had come out and were sitting on the pebbly beach, on a rug which Dirk had brought from the car.

'Father liked swimming, so I was lucky.'

'You wouldn't have been able to go with anyone else?'

'There wasn't anyone else to go with. The girls don't go swimming together, not alone. And as they can't go with a man—other than a father or brother, there isn't much chance. Of course, husbands sometimes take their wives with them, but mostly you only see men swimming—other than the tourists, of course.'

'It's an odd set-up,' he mused, and then, with a hint of amusement, 'Greece must be overflowing with nice innocent little virgins.'

She flushed.

'We're very well protected, as I've already told you.'

He regarded her with interest, his eyes flickering from her lovely face to her tiny breasts and then lower where they settled for a space before moving to her long slender legs and finally to her toes, with their lacquered nails, perfect in form to match the perfection of the rest of her body.

She fluttered him a glance; his eyes were serious and his brow creased in thought. He seemed possessed of an inner restlessness, which she detected despite the unemotional mask of his features. He gave a tiny sigh after a while and lay back, exposing his body to the sun. Perhaps now was the time to broach the subject of her visit to Greece, she thought, and after a small hesitation she said,

'Will it be all right if I go to see my father, Dirk?' The utterance nearly broke her heart, for if he should reply eagerly, making no protest, it would prove that he thought nothing about her at all.

He turned his head.

'Is that what you want?'

No—oh, *no*! It's you I want, she cried secretly.

'I told Father I'd be coming to see him, and you said I could, if you remember?'

'Yes, but I said Jenny would go with you. I understand it isn't the thing for you to travel alone?'

'It wouldn't have been, in the normal way. And Father will probably disapprove, but he'll understand that as I'm now English I can in fact travel alone.' She would feel utterly lost, she knew, and the flight would terrify her. It had been quite different when she had Charles and Dirk for company.

He smiled at her classing herself as English.

'If you want to go then I think it is advisable to wait until Jenny can go with you. She's going on holiday next week, isn't she?'

'Yes, for a fortnight.'

'Then you can go when she comes back.'

'She might not want to come with me.'

A pause, and then,

'We can ask her tomorrow when she comes to see you.'

Serra shook her head. If she waited for Jenny it would mean at least three weeks' delay, and Serra felt she must go sooner than that, for every day he had to be with her seemed to irritate her husband and she felt he would be better if he had a rest from her altogether.

'I want to go now—in a few days' time, that is.'

If he would only say she couldn't go ... because he would miss her....

'Well, if that's how you feel, I'll make the necessary arrangements tomorrow.'

She swallowed an ache in her throat, lowering her head to hide the moisture welling up in her eyes.

'Thank you,' she murmured, and he did not notice the stricken tone in her voice because he said,

'You don't mind flying alone?'

'No, I don't mind,' she returned in whispered accents. And so, three days later, Dirk and Jenny saw her off at the airport.

Jenny had naturally been surprised at this swift move on Serra's part, but she made no protest at all, a circumstance which did not do anything to ease the pain in Serra's heart. Even Jenny did not want her, she decided, indulging in a spate of self-pity.

Dirk had sent a cable to her father and he met her as she came off the plane. She looked well, and very happy, he declared, hugging her in front of everyone.

He had hired a taxi and they drove to the small white villa on the outskirts of Athens.

'Tell me everything?' he said eagerly when they were having tea on the patio, with the familiar exotic flowers blazing all around them. 'This house—you sent me photographs, but tell me of it.'

To her surprise she was not nearly so dejected as she had expected to be, for she loved her father and it was wonderful to see him again. It was also wonderful that Aunt Agni was away on a visit to her cousin, thought Serra, but naturally she made no comment about this.

'The house is a grand mansion,' she began. 'It stands in a beautiful park, and there are fountains and lawns and shady walks and statues—oh, many statues!'

'And you are happy, child?' His searching eyes ran over her. 'You have not made baby yet?'

The colour rushed to her face; she managed to stammer,

'No, n-not y-yet, Father.'

He shrugged, deprecatingly.

'These Englishmen—they take time! A Greek would have made baby the first night!'

Her colour subsided. She now wanted to laugh, but knew it was only because of nerves. What would Dirk say were he to hear her father talking like this?

'I have mentioned Jenny,' she said, changing the subject. 'She's very sweet and has taken me under her wing——'.

'Taken you under her wing? What is this—under wing?' He frowned in puzzlement and Serra said hastily,

'She takes me around, but—but Dirk does too, of course.'

His frown deepened.

'I understood Englishmen stayed with their wives all

176

the time. You mean, he sometimes goes out without you?'

'Were I married to Phivos,' she returned gently, 'I would have to tolerate his going out without me all the time.'

'Yes, certainly, but you are not married to Phivos. Your mother used to grumble when I went out without her and she would always remind me that, had she married an Englishman, she would never have been left alone.'

'Dirk has business to attend to.' She wished she hadn't made the slip, but as she had done so she now endeavoured to make excuses for her husband. 'He couldn't possibly be with me all the time.'

Another shrug.

'I hope you are happy, my child?'

'Perfectly, Father,' she lied, lowering her head.

'I think he should have come here with you.'

'That was impossible. As I've said, he has work to do.' Another lie. When would she stop?

'He didn't mind your coming alone? These Englishmen,' he added with a shake of his head. 'They do not seem to care what their wives do. I'm not sure, Serra, that I approve of this freedom the women have.'

'It is like that over there. All the women are free; they've achieved equality. It will come here in time.'

'Then I sincerely hope it is not in my time,' he declared emphatically, and something in the way he said that brought her head up with a jerk.

'You're not thinking of getting married again?' she gasped, horrified.

He looked away.

'I have met someone,' he muttered, half contrite, half challenging.

'But it isn't *done*.' He remained silent and she

added, 'You never remarry when once you've been widowed!'

'That's a sweeping statement, Serra. Sometimes people remarry.'

'All the family will be ashamed of you.'

'I daresay they will.'

'They won't accept this lady.'

'I'm sure you're right, my child.'

'And yet you're intending to marry her?'

'I've not definitely made up my mind—but she has a very excellent dowry. Tobacco fields and two houses. Two, what do you think of that?'

She looked thoroughly disgusted.

'It is a dreadful thing to get married again when once you're widowed, Father.'

He looked at her; she noticed the lines on his dark face, lines the sun had made ... and perhaps loneliness, she thought suddenly.

'What is this lady like?' she wanted to know, thinking of her own loneliness—which was nothing like that her father endured, because he had no one now that she had left him.

'You will like her, Serra,' he answered simply.

'I'm to meet her?'

'She comes to dinner this evening.'

Serra's eyes widened.

'Her parents allow this?'

A small silence and then,

'She too is widowed.'

Another silence as Serra digested this.

'What about her family? Do they approve?'

'On the contrary, they thoroughly disapprove.'

'Is she old?'

He smiled at that.

'She's thirty-eight. I expect you, my dear, consider

that old?'

'No. Dirk's twenty-eight,' she said irrelevantly. And, as her father did not speak, 'What's her name?'

'Maria.'

'Has she any children?'

'Of course. She has three.'

Serra frowned.

'Three children? They must be young?'

'Petros is eighteen, Anna is seventeen and Helena is almost fifteen.'

'Oh, dear, two girls. What about their dowries?' She shook her head emphatically. 'You can't marry a woman with two daughters, Father.'

'I have your dowry, remember, and as Maria has two houses we shall manage.'

'So Maria really has only one house with her dowry?'

'I suppose so, but,' he added, 'we do not need even that because I have this house.'

'Aunt Agni,' she began, when her father interrupted her to say,

'Aunt Agni is one of the reasons I'm considering this step. Life was bad enough before your marriage, but since——' He broke off and Serra thought he gave an inward shudder. 'She is a shrew, my dear, and I shall welcome the excuse of getting rid of her.'

'She still doesn't approve of my marrying Dirk?'

'She never approved of my marriage to your mother because she was English, remember.'

'No. She doesn't like the English, does she?'

'I'm afraid she doesn't. But what you do has nothing to do with her. I daresay she'd have grabbed at an Englishman, as a last resort, had she had the opportunity.'

No one had ever offered for Aunt Agni, and although Serra did not care for her at all she was in fact sorry for her, because to a Greek woman, marriage and children was her only aim.

'Do you love Maria?' she asked hesitantly at length.

'I like her very much. We don't fall madly in love, Serra, you know that.'

'Madly in love....' She spoke softly, and a little sadly. How had she come to fall madly in love with Dirk? It was a foolish thing to do and yet ... how could she help herself? Love just came, and it grew and grew until it filled your whole being.

'You're madly in love,' her father said, smiling at her. 'Anyone can see that.'

Anyone? Not Dirk. If he did ever see it, would it make him change towards her? Serra closed her eyes because of the ache of tears pressing against them. What was he doing now? she wondered, remembering the ravishing blonde he was with in Beirut. But if she were patient, as she had previously determined she would be, then some day Dirk might tire of all these lovely girls and want to settle down. Jenny was certain he would—eventually.

'And once I haven't all that competition I might just be able to make him notice me,' she whispered to herself.

To her surprise Serra liked Maria on sight. She was slim—which was unusual for a Greek woman who had been married for years—and her face was frank and softened with lines that could only be described as kind and compassionate. She seemed to like Serra, too, greeting her enthusiastically and immediately inquiring her about her husband and her home in England. And when dinner was over and Serra's father had gone to his room for a few moments Maria said, rather anxiously, Serra realized,

'Your father has told you we are thinking of getting married?' and when Serra nodded, 'Many people will frown on us, but, my dear, we are both very lonely.'

'Yes, I think I understand,' Serra murmured, feeling a little shy because of the confiding manner of the older woman.

'The opinion of others worries us, but we like each other and feel we can be happy together.' A small pause. 'You, Serra—what would you think if we married?'

Raising frank eyes to Maria's face, Serra said,

'When Father first mentioned it I was—well, a little horrified, as you can imagine. But on thinking about it, and after meeting you——' She broke off and smiled. 'I would like my father to marry you.'

Maria leant forward and took Serra's small hand in hers.

'Thank, you, Serra,' she whispered huskily. 'Thank you very much indeed. I think we shall not take notice of our critical relatives. We shall take the course that will bring us both happiness.'

Serra recalled that her father had not been quite sure about the marriage, but when he came out to them on the patio and Maria told him what his daughter had said he smiled and the faint expression of strain and uncertainty which had been with him all through dinner faded away as he said,

'Then you at least would not condemn us?'

'Maria has told you what I've said, Father. I would like you to get married—and I'm very sure you'll be happy together,' and she added, 'The relations will come round in the end, I have no doubt of that.'

Serra had told her father that she would be staying a few weeks, and although he registered surprise he made no comment. He would never understand those

Englishmen, his expression seemed to say. Serra wrote to Dirk, and to Mrs Morgan and, later, when she knew Jenny would have returned from her holiday she wrote to her too. Jenny wrote back, advising Serra to remain in Greece a little while longer. She gave no reason, her letter being strangely guarded and, misunderstanding, Serra wept bitter tears when she read it. Dirk did not want her to return....

Maria and Elias were married quietly at the church in the village where Maria lived. Serra walked with other girls of about her own age, each carrying a brown candle about two foot long, and decorated with a wide ribbon bow at the top. Despite the general disapproval everyone turned out and it was a merry procession that walked up the hill to the pretty white church, where the bearded priest was waiting. Inside the church chattering went on apace during the ceremony, and now and then some young man would ask the priest to stop the service while he took a snapshot of the couple, who would pose, smiling, one on either side of the priest. Then the ceremony would continue —until the next interruption.

The wedding feast was held in the orchard of Maria's house, the tables, very long and draped with snow-white cloths, literally sagging with food. The wine flowed and the bride and groom sat on chairs and gave out wedding biscuits to the guests.

Many people talked to Serra, asking about her husband and her home. The Greek girls all asked her if she were in love and she answered truthfully. No one thought to ask if her husband were also in love.

A fortnight after the wedding Elias asked Serra when she was going home. He was clearly troubled now and Serra knew she must be thinking of going back to England. Yet Jenny's most recent letter, received only a week ago, again advised Serra to remain in Greece.

'Next week, perhaps,' she answered her father, trying to hide her dejection. How could she go home when her husband did not want her? He had answered her letters, it was true, but in cool impersonal tones.

'Perhaps?' frowned Elias.

'I l-like it here, Father,' she stammered.

'But your husband has plenty of money, so you can come again—just as often as you like.'

She nodded.

'I'll go into Athens and find out when there is a plane,' she began, but he interrupted her.

'There are plenty of planes. Serra, are you happy with your husband?'

'Of course! What a question!' Was she convincing? Perhaps, for her father did not pursue the matter further.

On setting out the following day for Athens, where she would arrange her flight home, Serra told her father not to expect her back for tea, as she intended spending the afternoon on the Acropolis.

Having arranged to leave Greece on the coming Saturday she strolled towards the Plaka, her unhappiness a leaden weight now that her decision was finally made. Somehow, at the back of her mind, there had flickered a hope that Dirk was missing her, and that he would write telling her she must come home. But two long months had passed and Serra at last admitted it was a forlorn hope that she cherished. What must her future be? There was only a lonely void ahead, for she had no desire for the carefree round of pleasure in which she had originally expected to indulge.

Conflicting thoughts intruded to confuse her mind.

That new maturity which had entered into Dirk; his sister's confidence that he would soon change his wild ways. There was Dirk's softness on several occasions; there were his kisses and that admission that he had enjoyed being with her. Serra recalled her glowing confidence on the night of the dinner party, and her happiness the following day ... until that moment when Dirk had said in a hard inflexible tone,

'No one will ever reform me.'

Serra's eyes flickered. Was it merely obstinacy on her husband's part? Basically he was strong of character and will, and it would be natural for him to experience anger that his sister should be endeavouring to 'mould' him. And that was what she *was* endeavouring to do. Hadn't Jenny expressed the hope that, one day, she might have the sort of brother she wanted?

Having reached the Plaka Serra repeatedly glanced upwards to the great limestone rock, dropping sheer on all sides except the west, and each time her eyes were raised she felt a stab of pain in her heart as she remembered the last time she had been on the Acropolis. It was stupid to go there today, but a compulsion over which she had no control had been with her since her waking hour, when she knew she was going into Athens to make arrangements for a return to the husband who did not want her. The ancient rock had always drawn her, wrapped as it was in a veil of pagan mystery. For although much was known of the ceremonies and rites which were enacted in the temples, there was much still remaining obscure.

Taking the steep path through the cypress grove—the approach to the Acropolis which most tourists missed owing to their being driven there by coach or taxi—Serra entered from a different point from that through which the ancient Panathenaic processions passed so long ago—the beautiful Propylaea with its marble steps and magnificent Doric columns.

She wandered about for a while and then, strolling over to the Parthenon, she sat down on one of the steps, her mind naturally filled with the dramatic events of that other occasion, the occasion when Dirk entered her life, subsequently to become the man who would lift her from the restrictive customs of her father's country and transport her to the freedom that had been her mother's heritage as a girl.

Tears filled her eyes as she recalled one momentous incident after another. Dirk's promise, which she feared he would not keep; their wedding day, so quiet, lacking the pomp and gay abandon that accompanied that of her father and Maria only a short while ago. Yet Serra had not minded the quiet wedding because it meant escape. Then the visit to Beirut and her two scrapes which had made Dirk so angry. There was the journey to England and the meeting with her mother-in-law——

Serra braked her reflections at that point, for she squirmed at the vision of herself, smothered in soot and cobwebs, facing the elegant astonished woman whom she had previously heard refer to her son's wife as an oddity.

An hour passed and still Serra sat there, chiding herself for her dejection and telling herself she was lucky to have married a rich Englishman, and that she should not expect more than what Dirk had originally promised. She stood up at last; the sun was beginning to drop and the temples were bathed in the ethereal transience of an Eastern sunset, their columns and pediments and entablatures sprinkled with a lacy quivering splendour of copper and gold and russet-bronze. A breeze fluttered in from the west to stir

Serra's hair and fan her cheeks, lightly touching them with a rosy hue. The one or two people strolling about put up their coat collars, but Serra turned her face into the wind, feeling it drive through her hair after gently caressing her brow.

Suddenly she blinked, and her heart seemed to swing right over. What hallucination was this! A hand went automatically to her stomach—butterflies! —and her legs felt weak, just as on that other occasion.

Having spotted her, he stood for one profound moment and looked at her, then strode towards the mighty temple, and the small trembling figure that was his wife. His manner was confident, his approach swift, as if every separating second irked now that his tardy decision was made. And yet on reaching her he hesitated, and she saw with wonderment that he found speech difficult.

The few people still remaining on the Acropolis had drifted towards the Propylaea, through which they presently disappeared. And still Dirk stood there, looking down at his wife with infinite tenderness and love in his dark eyes. His gaze was searching, as if he would seek an answer to his silent question. Her swift trembling smile was that answer and a little laugh of triumph escaped him. Serra could only stare, spellbound, dazzled by this miracle.

'You have come ... you have come to me——' The rest was smothered in a kiss, tender and warm and ardent. His strong arms embraced her and she nestled her head against his shoulder, the questions flitting through her mind ignored in this intimate moment of ecstasy. He kissed her again and again, as if he would make up for all those lost days and weeks of uncertainty. But after a while he released her and, taking her hand, led her to the spot where she had been sitting—on that first day—a moment before Charles had cheerily asked her to remain still until he had taken his snapshot. They sat close and Dirk told her of his struggle, of his reluctance to settle down and be the family man.

'Yet I have known for some time, my love, that I was finding you devastatingly attractive, but I fought it and fought it—right up till yesterday I fought, but at last I knew that all I wanted was to love my wife and to be loved by her.' He turned his head and she caught her breath at the wealth of love in his expression. 'I know you care—I saw it in your smile just now—so I have my wish, for I love you with all my heart——' He broke off, emotionally affected as she would never have believed he could be. 'I bless the day I found you, my little Serra, here on the steps of Athena's Temple.' His mouth caressed her cheek in a way that set her pulses tingling; she turned her face and gave him her lips.

'Yesterday, when you decided to love me——' she began a little while later.

'Decided?' He slanted her an amused glance. 'That's a unique way of putting it! I've loved you some time, my sweet.'

She laughed shakily, still a little shy, and overwhelmed by this stupendous happening that had changed her whole life in a matter of minutes.

'Yesterday, when you discovered you wanted me— why didn't you write and tell me to come home? I was coming home on Saturday anyway,' she added, curling her small hand round his.

'The most sensible and practical thing was for me to write,' he agreed. 'But having at last seen the light—or rather, admitted to seeing it—I had a sudden desire to have a holiday with you in Athens; a honeymoon, my love, and so I simply booked myself a seat on today's plane and here I am. On my arrival I immediately took a taxi to your father's house and he told me you would be here.' His fingers moved caressingly across her hand before he lifted it to his lips. 'What made you stay away so long?' he asked, keeping her hand close to his mouth.

'It was Jenny——' Serra stopped, afraid of what she had let slip.

'Jenny?' frowningly.

A pause and then a reluctant,

'Jenny wrote advising me to stay here a little while longer. I thought it was because she had decided you were happier without me,' she added, even though she now guessed at the reason for her sister-in-law's advice. Dirk had required a little more time to get round to admitting the truth—that he could not live without his wife.

'So Jenny had a hand in it after all,' he mused, a tiny glint in his eye. 'And I thought I was doing it all myself.'

'You're not vexed?' she faltered, twisting her head to look into his face.

'No, my darling, I'm not vexed. Jenny knew better than I, apparently,' and the glint was replaced by an expression of infinite tenderness. 'Everyone's happy. You—because I see the love in your eyes, me, because I have my lovely wife, and Jenny because her brother's all nicely reformed.'

Serra leant her head against her husband's shoulder and his cheek pressed lovingly on her brow. A hush fell on the sacred sanctuary. The sun was dropping rapidly and soon these, the world's loveliest buildings, would be 'violet-crowned'. But for this fleeting twilight interlude the vivid colours of crimson and flame prevailed. Clouds blazed above the hallowed site, and far away

Mount Lykabettus melted into their fiery depths. With the passing moments the earth continued to turn, beckoning the sun to another hemisphere, and gradually the purple shadows closed in on the couple sitting, quite alone, on the steps of the temple.

'My darling——' The words were whispered, for the hush was holy and profound. 'Are you getting cold?' Dirk drew her closer as he spoke, and tilting her chin he touched her lips with his.

'No, I'm not getting cold, but I suppose we should be going.' A deep and contented sigh fell on the silent air. 'I'm so happy I could cry.'

'My love, I hope you won't do any such thing.'

She laughed instead and a gentle hand urged her to her feet. Dirk held her in his arms, looking down at her with tender emotion, and faintly shaking his head, as if unable to believe he had been so long accepting the fact that his wife held more attraction for him than all the other girls put together.

'My love——' He bent to kiss her and she responded, with shy hesitancy at first, until his ardour awakened the new emotion and she surrendered her lips, so that he was aware of her love, and her desire. 'We'll have a honeymoon, beginning tonight!' His voice was hoarse yet filled with a wealth of tenderness too and happiness and gratitude surged through Serra's whole body. 'Shall we spend the entire time here, or would you like to go to Beirut again?'

Her eyes sparkled.

'I'd very much like to go again,' she answered eagerly.

His eyes suddenly kindled with amusement as recollection swept in. She read his thoughts and a tinkling laugh fell like sweet music on the silent sanctuary.

'I'll have you to take care of me this time,' she reminded him with a hint of mischief.

'This time ... and for always,' and he tucked her arm in his and they moved in the purple dusky silence towards the Propylaea. Overhead the stars were beginning to light the vast vault of the sky, and behind them the great temple and its pagan gods were wrapped in slumber.

Mills & Boon
Best Seller Romances

The very best of Mills & Boon
brought back for those of you
who missed reading them when they
were first published.
There are three other Best Seller Romances
for you to collect this month.

SHOW ME
by Janet Dailey

It was seven years since Tanya had seen her husband Jake, but their young son needed a father and now she had asked him to come home. But even in the circumstances she was not prepared for the hostility and suspicion with which Jake treated her. Was it worth trying to save their marriage?

TAKE WHAT YOU WANT
by Anne Mather

Sophie was only a teenager, but she knew she would never love, had never loved, anyone but her stepbrother Robert. But her whole family, including Robert, disapproved, and hoped she would get over the feeling. Were they right – or was Sophie?

THE SIN OF CYNARA
by Violet Winspear

Carol was determined to do the best she could for little fatherless Teri, even if it meant going to Italy and begging from his father's family. But Carol had visualised a kindly grandfather – not the child's uncle, the formidable Baróne Rudolph Falcone, whose scarred face matched his unrelenting attitude to her . . .

If you have difficulty in obtaining any of these books through your local paperback retailer, write to:
Mills & Boon Reader Service
P.O. Box 236, Thornton Road, Croydon, Surrey, CR9 3RU

How to join in a whole new world of romance

It's very easy to subscribe to the Mills & Boon Reader Service. As a regular reader, you can enjoy a whole range of special benefits. Bargain offers. Big cash savings. Your own free Reader Service newsletter, packed with knitting patterns, recipes, competitions, and exclusive book offers.

We send you the very latest titles each month, postage and packing free – no hidden extra charges. There's absolutely no commitment – you receive books for only as long as you want.

We'll send you details. Simply send the coupon – or drop us a line for details about the Mills & Boon Reader Service Subscription Scheme.
Post to: Mills & Boon Reader Service, P.O. Box 236, Thornton Road, Croydon, Surrey CR9 3RU, England.
*Please note: READERS IN SOUTH AFRICA please write to: Mills & Boon Reader Service of Southern Africa, Private Bag X3010, Randburg 2125, S. Africa.

Please send me details of the Mills & Boon Subscription Scheme.

NAME (Mrs/Miss) _____ EP3

ADDRESS _____

_____

COUNTY/COUNTRY _____ POST/ZIP CODE _____
BLOCK LETTERS, PLEASE

Mills & Boon
the rose of romance